MALE NURSE

Joe Kamm

ISBN: 1508918309
ISBN 13: 9781508918301

For all the people out there struggling with addiction. You are strong and you are powerful, no matter what they say.

PART 1

CHAPTER ONE

8:30am. It's so hot. I step out of the hospital and I can feel a sticky layer of sweat forming on my skin beneath my scrubs. My long sleeve undershirt doesn't help but it's the only way to hide the track marks.

I walk to the elevator at the parking garage.

I nervously check my pockets as I wait with a small crowd of people who are all anxious to get home and get to bed.

I reach into my right pocket and feel my wallet, my keys, and a few unopened alcohol pads. In my left pocket I feel my cigarettes, my lighter, a few loose Percocets, and a syringe.

The doors open and I step inside.

Everyone in the elevator is either staring at the door or looking down at their phones. I reach into my shirt pocket and feel the vials. They make a clinking sound as they rub together but no one notices. I roll them between my fingers like rosary beads. We all get off on the fifth floor, which is reserved for employee parking.

Everyone gets in their cars and drives away without any goodbyes.

Night shift people are not the friendliest bunch.

I tell myself that I'm going to wait until I get home to indulge in any substances but I never do. Every morning I stop at the same gas station and get a big Budweiser for the ride home.

I bring the beer out to my car then drive around to the air pump machine and park. I fill the huge, plastic coffee cup that I keep in my cup holder to the brim with the cold beer then I take two Percocets out of my pocket and swallow them with the first drink. The first drink is always the best. The hope is that the pills will come into full bloom right after I get home, shoot up, and take Godzilla for a walk so I can prolong the high until it's time to go to sleep.

I've got the timing down to an art.

I live on a tiny little island near downtown Tampa, Florida called Davis Island. My apartment complex is a one-story building with six small apartments arranged around a courtyard. There are six parking spots behind the building and I always say a silent prayer before turning onto my street that one will be available.

Got one!

I'm so anxious to get to my shot that I do a light jog to the door and a vial almost falls out of my pocket.

I hear Godzilla barking his tiny-dog bark. He's a fat little Pug that was never intended to live in such a hot climate. Poor guy.

I open the door and he scratches my legs as I walk to the fridge to get another beer.

"Calm down, Godzilla. One minute, buddy. I know, I love you too."

I can see a puddle of piss by my bedroom door but I decide to ignore it. I have more important things to do. I wouldn't be able to hold it for thirteen hours either.

I sit at my desk and lay the vials, the alcohol pads, and the syringe out in front of me. I open one of the desk drawers and pull out an ACE bandage. I open the syringe and an alcohol pad. I clean the top of one of the vials of Dilaudid and draw up two milliliters of the thick liquid. It's way too thick for those little insulin syringes most junkies use. I wish I could use those needles. I pull up my sleeve and wrap the bandage tightly around my bicep and then pin the loose end underneath my elbow as I rest my arm on the desk. Godzilla is still clawing at my legs. I wipe my bulging skin with the alcohol pad and then align the needle with the vein. I bury the bevel of the needle beneath the first layer of skin then bend the needle slightly upward as it slides into the blood vessel. This is a trick I learned to avoid "rolling veins", as the amateurs call them.

Here it comes.

Not the moment the drug enters my system. The moment I see the blood shoot back up into the syringe. That's my favorite moment. When you're standing on the edge looking down.

I lift up my elbow to release the tension on the bandage and then push the plunger.

I feel it in the back of my neck.

I taste it.

I smell it.

All of my aches and pains and fears and concerns turn to euphoria.

At this moment I'm enlightened, I'm centered, at peace, at one with the world and everyone in it, connected to everything but not attached to anything. I'm the living embodiment of every self-help cliché in the book. It feels so, fucking, good.

I pull out the needle and wrap the bandage around my arm to stop the bleeding. The bandage is stained with over a dozen patches of dried blood.

I pull out a canvass from behind the desk.

This might sound morbid, and honestly I'm not sure why I do it.

I prop the canvas against the wall and go get a small glass of water.

I dip the tip of the needle into the water and draw up a small amount and then I spray the water mixed with the blood onto the canvas.

It looks like bright red spray paint when it's wet but it dries into a dark maroon.

I've been doing this for a while now and the canvas is almost completely covered and I'm not sure when or why I started.

I tuck the canvas back behind the desk then go and grab Godzilla's leash and the beer that I opened earlier.

I walk back outside holding the leash in one hand and the beer and a lit cigarette in the other. God only knows what my neighbors think when they see me drinking beer this early in the morning. With the beer, the Percocet, and now the Dilaudid in my system, I could honestly give a shit.

I walk down the street with my head held high, nodding at people as they leave their houses on their way to work. They nod back nervously, like they're not sure if I'm going to rob their house after they leave.

After the walk, I clean up the puddle of piss and take a shower.

After the shower, I shoot up again and put away my empty vials in the kitchen cabinet. I save all of the empty vials and on my days off work I fill each one with a milliliter of normal saline, swirl them around, and then inject the liquid intramuscularly. Only then I can throw them out.

I usually put all of the vials and used syringes inside empty beer bottles and throw them in the dumpster by my apartment.

There have been times that I have been drunk and extremely desperate for a shot and re-claimed beer bottles from the dumpster to get the vials back to try and get more out of them.

It usually doesn't work and I usually regret it the next day.

After I put my vials away I go into my medicine cabinet and take a handful of Benadryl and an Ambien then I lie on the couch and watch a movie.

I cancelled my cable a month ago so I am stuck watching movies that I rent from a DVD kiosk in front of the Walgreens down the street. They never have anything good but I'm usually so fucked up that it doesn't matter what's on the screen. I just need the comfort of human voices.

The pills kick in and I can feel myself nodding off.

I smoke one last cigarette then Godzilla curls his fat little body up on my pillow beside my head and we fall asleep.

I have been in this apartment for three months and never once have I slept in my bed.

The bed reminds me of her.

It was *our* bed.

CHAPTER TWO

I was a functional drug addict and alcoholic when we were together but after the split I went downhill fast. Really fast. Every day now it seems like I discover a new bottom. I'm not sure if I'm subconsciously punishing myself for the way that I treated her or if I'm just a selfish, self-indulgent asshole.

She kept me afloat all those years and what did I give her in return? Shit. Lies. Scumbag excuses.

I wake up and Godzilla is standing on my chest snorting into my face. It's hot in my apartment and my blanket is damp with sweat.

I keep myself hidden in the shadows as I step outside with Godzilla.

I'm in no shape to see any strangers right now.

I have to get ready for work again.

I stop by my neighbor Tom's apartment and knock on his door.

"Hey, Tom! Open up, man, it's me, Jack."

Tom doesn't work nights, he just prefers to sleep during the day and stay up all night because of the heat.

Tom doesn't work at all, actually. He's forty years old and probably never has. He comes from a wealthy family and I guess they just kind of let him do whatever he wants.

He's a Goodell, if that means anything to you. Like, as in, the Goodell family that owns half of this town. He must have really pissed them off to end up living in these shitty apartments.

He opens the door without a shirt on. His potbelly is covered in a layer of short, black hair. His eyes aren't even open.

"Jack. What's up, man?"

"Do you think I could get a couple Roxies from you? I'll pay you. I'm all out and my hip is killing me."

I do have an old hip injury but it doesn't hurt much. I pretend to have hip pain, he pretends to have back pain, he knows that I'm lying, and I know that he's lying. Whatever, it's what we do.

"I got you, man. Let me go get you one. I'm running low."

He walks over to a coffee table beside his futon and picks up a cellophane baggie with three little blue pills in it. He takes one out and hands it to me.

"Thank you so much. I'm working tonight."

"Are you off tomorrow night?"

"Yeah. Why? You wanna hang out?"

"Yeah, Bobby's comin' over, we're just gonna get fucked up."

"I'll stop by."

"Why don't you check out one of the pill-mills, man? You have money and insurance. You can get as much as you want. I'll buy enough off of you so you break even."

"Too lazy, I guess. Maybe soon."

"Take it easy, man. I'm goin' back to bed."

"Thanks again."

I go inside and break the Roxy in half. I'll take half now and half before I go inside the hospital.

It's important that I'm on top of my game when I walk in and get my assignment.

Before I leave I indulge in my worst habit, which is checking up on my ex on Facebook. It hurts so bad every time but I keep doing it for some reason. Just about every day I find myself on there looking at her pictures. I can't stop.

Her name is Michelle, by the way. She moved up north to Jersey after we split up and is dating some other guy now. An engineer, I think. He's good looking and clean. Healthy. Stable. Responsible. They smile a lot in their pictures and their smiles seem genuine.

I scroll through a new batch of pictures of them having a wonderful time at the Jersey Shore.

I don't know why I do this to myself.

I crush up the second half of the Roxy and snort it on my console before I walk in. I walk up to the nurse's station and look at my patient assignment. Not bad. As long as I have at least two patients who have orders for regular doses of Dilaudid I'm good. If I don't, things get tricky.

If you don't have patients with heavy narcotic orders you have a few options.

One option is to trade.

The patients that are in a lot of pain are the most demanding and most nurses will gladly give them up. The other patients with heavy narcotic orders are the drug seekers and they are even easier to take off peoples' hands. How do you tell a fellow nurse that you want their most difficult patient and not seem like a desperate drug addict? You can either take the high road and tell them that they look tired and you want to help, or you tell them that you had that patient the night before and it would just be easier if you had the same patients. They never question me. The only nurses who refuse to give up their patients are the fellow addicts. This is a bigger problem than you would think.

Another option is to get new orders. Doctors hate to be bothered at night, so this is what you do:

You get into work early. You ask all of your patients if they're in pain. If any of them say yes, you call their doctor and tell them that whatever they have ordered isn't working. Then you tell the doctor that the patient said that Morphine makes them itch. The last thing the doctor wants is to get calls all night about a patient whose pain isn't being controlled or whose meds are causing uncomfortable side effects. Once you tell them about the itching with Morphine they will order Dilaudid, two-to-four milligrams, every four-to-six hours, as needed for pain. They always do.

So how do I steal the drugs? It's pretty simple.

After I get the order for Dilaudid every four-to-six hours, the Pyxis machine will let me take a vial out every four hours. So that's what I take. Whether the patient asks for it or not. I watch the clock and remove the drugs the very minute the machine will allow me to. This optimizes the amount that I will be able to remove during my twelve-hour shift.

If the patient asks for pain meds I always have some in my pocket. A lot of it. They're usually thrilled with how prompt I am. So, who is the victim? The insurance company? The hospital? Fuck them.

My patients for tonight look good. Lots of drug seekers and people in pain. And just my luck, after I get report one of them is due for a shot. I look at his chart and see that he hasn't been asking for any. Perfect. I take a vial out of the machine, grab a syringe, and go to the restroom.

Intravenous Dilaudid is great. The problem, however, is that the high is short-lived. Wonderful, but short-lived. I save the intravenous stuff for after work. While I work I prefer intramuscular. I clean off a little spot of skin on my left deltoid with an alcohol pad and then jam the needle into the muscle. I push the solution in slowly. It stings but in a good way. The thing about intramuscular is, it comes on slow but lasts longer. Much better for work.

I shoot the contents of the vial into my arm, make sure that I'm not bleeding, and then begin my shift.

On the floor where I work, each nurse gets their own Patient Care Technician to help with their patients. The PCT's can make or break your night. I have Jessica tonight. This is good and bad.

Jessica, like 99% of all PCT's, is studying to be a nurse. She's probably the best PCT we have. Unfortunately, I fucked her a few times last week and I'm pretty sure that she thinks we're an item now.

I'm really only into her ass to be quite honest. She's Puerto Rican. It's huge. I'm not sure why I added the Puerto Rican part. I guess when you're describing a girl with a huge ass you can picture it a lot of different ways. If I add that she's Puerto Rican it gives you a clearer picture of the type of huge ass I'm talking about. If a white girl has a huge ass she is most likely obese. This is not necessarily the case with Latina women. Aside from the sexy, huge ass I'm not interested in her. She's kind of crazy. Again, and I'm sorry to say this, but I think the fact that she's Latina gives you a clearer picture of the kind of crazy she is. The jealous kind. The kind that always seems to be on the edge of turning physically violent.

She's leaning over the desk that I plan on using tonight, arching her back. I know that she knows that I'm watching her and I know already that I'm going to end up fucking her again after work.

Being a male nurse has a million perks, but the number one benefit has to be the women. The nurses. There are so many of them and so many of them are lonely. You would be amazed at how many nurses are either divorced, getting divorced, or cheating on their husbands with someone in the hospital. I'm telling you, you would be blown away. I'm not even that good looking. I mean, I'm not bad looking, but nowhere near good looking enough to be able to sleep with the women that I have. Not even close. They sleep with me because, well, I'm there. You would also be amazed at how many nurses turn into lesbians during their nursing careers. These are women with husbands and kids, the whole deal. Women who never looked at another woman sexually their entire life. They start working as a nurse, some butchy chick starts giving them the attention that they're not getting at home, next thing you know, lesbian. Happens all the time. It's sort of like the hospital version of prison gay. Gay by default.

My best friend in the hospital is a lesbian. Her name is Myka. I'm pretty sure she's the real deal, though. Not prison lesbian but real lesbian. She has hooked up with at least two married women that I know of. I know this because I make her tell and re-tell the stories over and over until she cuts me off.

The night goes by smoothly. Jessica and I don't talk much but the sexual energy is there. I took a few Adderalls from the Pyxis so I'm a little amped up and feeling frisky.

When my shift is over I ask her if she needs a ride home. She calls the guy who was going to pick her up, probably her boyfriend, and tells him that she doesn't need a ride anymore. I make it out with three full vials of Dilaudid and a couple Adderalls.

Jessica, along with all of the other women that have found their way into my apartment, thinks that I am just an alcoholic. I never let them know about the other substances. If they see me really fucked up, they just think I'm a drunk. I can live with that.

Want to hear a crazy double standard?

If I find out that a girl has a drug or alcohol problem I'm immediately turned off. But I swear to you, the fact that the girls at my job know that I'm an alcoholic makes them want me more. I have no idea why. I have been told on more than one occasion that "so and so" told them that I was a raging alcoholic and that is what made them interested in me. Maybe it's not that way with women in general but it is with nurses. They are naturally nurturing people. Codependent. They see me and they think, "yeah, he's kind of cute," then they find out I'm an alcoholic and they think "hmm, there must be more to him than meets the eye. He must be suffering, poor thing, maybe I can help."

It sucks, but it's true. I believe that if I weren't an addict I wouldn't do nearly as well with women.

I take Jessica home, fuck her senseless, mostly doggy style, shoot up in the bathroom, and then drive her home.

I stop by McDonalds on the way home and it's past eleven so I get a twenty-piece chicken nugget meal for myself and a six-piece nugget meal for Godzilla.

We eat then we sleep.

No work tonight.

Thank God.

CHAPTER THREE

I wake up and realize that I shot up all of my Dilaudid before I passed out on the couch. I also tapped out the empty vials. Technically, I should be dead.

I look through my desk and my medicine cabinet. I find a few Benzodiazepines, some muscle relaxers, some "non-narcotic" pain relievers, and a sleeping pill. I'm going to need opiates and I'm off for three days. Occasionally I do get so desperate that I call my job and beg to pick up a shift. They ask around other floors and usually find a spot for me. I need the hospital way more than it needs me.

I stole drugs on my first shift ever as a nurse. Actually, I wasn't even a nurse yet, come to think of it. I had graduated and been hired at the hospital but I was working under another nurse while I waited to take my test.

I carried two Percocets into a patient's room and they told me that they only wanted one.

I didn't even consider for a second putting that pill back. Not even for a second. Going back even further, I can tell you the first time I ever took an opiate.

I was in high school and I hurt my knee skating. I found a bottle of prescription pain pills in my step-dad's medicine cabinet. I read the label and saw that they were for pain so I took one and went back to my room. I was reading a book about Native Americans at the time. I was into hallucinogenic drugs and I was learning about shamans like every other stoner high school kid. I had a desk chair in my room that rocked. I sat in my chair, propped my feet up on my bed, and read my book while rocking back and forth. The drug kicked in and I had never felt happier or more content. That's all there is to that story. I sat there and read until the drugs wore off. I will never forget that feeling.

But back to my first day as a nurse.

I put the pill in my pocket, brought it home, and took it with a sip of cold beer. I slept like a baby. The next day I did the same thing.

I started off just taking the leftovers but after a couple days I was actively pursuing the drugs and manipulating people to get them.

Needles were tough at first since I was scared to death of shots. I never had a problem giving them but I had a tendency to pass out when receiving them. The first time I put a needle into my own skin I was scared that I was going to pass out and someone was going to find me with a needle sticking out of my ass. But by that time my need for drugs had surpassed my fear. I got used to it very fast. Now, I love the needle. I crave the feeling of it. I find myself daydreaming about it sometimes like some strange masochistic fantasy that I'm sure has some deep psychological roots in my childhood.

I have to stop thinking about it now. I need to figure out how I'm going to get enough pills to last me till my next shift.

I do know where the nearest pill-mill is.

I guess I could go.

Fuck. Why not?

A pill-mill is something that only exists in Florida. As far as I know. It's a doctor's office attached to a pharmacy, usually in a shady neighborhood, where you can get scripts for whatever you want and then fill the scripts right there. They deal mostly in cash.

The pill-mill that I know of is in a small building that looks like it was once a convenience store. It's in a really shitty part of town. A lot of factories and warehouses around.

I see several people hanging out in the parking lot as I pull up. Some of them are talking on phones, others are huddled together in little groups. At least four of the people that I see loitering outside have crutches, which I'm sure they don't need.

I get suspicious looks from the parking lot people as I walk up to the glass door.

I step inside and it's almost too much. I almost just leave.

The waiting room is packed. All of the seats are filled and the rest of the room is crowded with people who are rocking and fidgeting. What really gets me is all of the people with kids. The moms and dads that are here with their sons and daughters. The kids look so happy just to be out with their parents. They laugh and play games on cell phones and ask questions like "Why are there so many people here, Mommy?" or "Do all of these people have back pain like you, Daddy?"

I feel nauseous and I'm not sure if it's because of what I'm seeing or because I'm in the early stages of withdrawal.

I have to stick it out.

I get to the glass window and the woman tells me that it's going to be a hundred bucks and that I have to pay in cash. Of course there's an ATM machine in the corner of the waiting room.

I withdraw the hundred bucks, pay her, and then fill out a sheet that I know that no one is going to read.

How bad is your pain on a scale of one to ten? Ten.

Any surgeries or procedures in the past ten years? Yes. Left hip surgery with severe nerve damage following an automobile accident.

Are you currently taking any medications? Hmmm. No.

I stand among the crowd of people and listen to their conversations. They are all telling stories about bad backs and bad feet or shoulders. They are all such poor, suffering victims. I have to remind myself several times that I am one of them. I am no better. I'm sure they are all thinking the same things about me. There is only one reason you go to a place like this and that is to get a shitload of pain pills without too many questions.

Finally, they call my name and I go back.

The nurses and assistants look like hell. Like they've seen and heard it all. I try to make small talk and get "save your breath" looks from all of them. Pretty much everything that comes out of a drug addict's mouth is bullshit and they know it. Having people lie to your face for eight hours every day must be exhausting.

What am I talking about, it *is* exhausting. Just because I work at a hospital doesn't mean I don't deal with the same thing. Sometimes it's worse. I work mostly on a neurology floor where a good portion of my patients are there having completely unnecessary surgeries and who are hopeless drug addicts just like me. The blind caring for the blind.

When I got in the car accident that shattered my hip I spent ten days in the same hospital, on the same floor, where I now work. They were very liberal with the meds. In fact, after I left I started going through withdrawals but I had no idea at that time what withdrawals were. I went to the surgeon several times and explained to him what was going on and he never once put the pieces together and realized that I was having a hard time coming off the drugs. He diagnosed me with some made up nerve condition and sent me for injections in my spine. Of course the only things that actually relieved the symptoms were drugs. Opiates to be more specific.

The car accident was the beginning of the end for my ex and me. My drinking was already out of control but the accident is what gave me a taste for the opiates. The opiates turned me from a good-natured drunk to the deceitful, selfish, liar that I am today.

A woman takes my vital signs when I get into the exam room and I don't even bother talking. When I go to see a doctor I have this insatiable urge to let everyone know that I'm a nurse and I'm not sure why. I do want to tell the woman who is taking my vitals but I decide not to. Instead I think about fucking her on the exam table. Her tits are so big that it looks like her scrub top is about to rip open.

She catches me staring at her chest and I look at one of the anatomy posters on the wall. It's a picture of a human spine. At the bottom is an advertisement for a drug that targets nerve pain.

The doctor walks in.

Oh my God. What a fucking douche bag.

He's young and tan and full of chemical energy. I wonder immediately how a medical doctor ends up in a place like this. I'm sure the money is great, but, come on. I picture him sitting out behind the building between seeing patients doing lines of coke in his BMW. He talks to some smitten girl on the phone who is so happy that this "doctor" is interested in her.

He walks up to me and pretends to read the paper that I filled out in the waiting room. He nods his head as he reads. Then, he looks up at me.

"Jack. So, you've got some pain, huh?"

"Yeah, it's my hip. I got in a car accident a while back and had a lot of nerve damage. The pain has been getting worse. I'm on my feet all day at work. I've tried pretty much every medication out there but nothing has helped. A friend of mine suggested that I come see you guys."

"You came to the right place, my man." He looks at me with an intense look. Like he's about to say something that's going to blow my mind. "This is what we're gonna do, Jack. You've got this pain, right, this pain that you can't control no matter how hard you try. Am I right?" He puts his hands on my shoulders and looks me in the eye. "We are going to make that pain your bitch, Jack. Do you understand me?" He smiles and expects me to smile back, so I do. "We are going to get on top of that pain, Jack! With pain like this you can't wait until it gets bad, man, then it's too late! We're going to get right on top of that pain and make it your bitch! We are going to control that pain so that it doesn't control you. Do you understand what I'm saying, Jack?"

"Sounds good, Doc."

He nods his head proudly.

"You sure have a lot of patients out there." I say, as he writes something in my chart.

"You came on a bad day. Never come here on a day when unemployment or disability checks are issued. Just a word of advice."

I picture all of the other people who pass through this exam room who probably get this same speech. I imaging that most people lose their apprehension and feelings of guilt after a "doctor" tells them that they are doing the right thing. I pretend to be impressed by this man who I truly believe is the worst person I've ever met.

"Yeah, I understand. It's so nice to meet a doctor who *gets* it, you know."

"You're gonna be just fine, Jack. I'm writing you a prescription for some very strong pills. This is what you need, Jack. This is how we're going to get ahead of things. You are going to take these at the first sign of pain and every four hours afterwards. After the pain is under control, you can start to cut back. How's that sound?"

"Great."

He pats me on the back.

I look down and see him scribble the word Roxicodone.

Roxicodone, or Roxies as we call them, are thirty milligrams of immediate release oxycodone. They come in little blue pills. If you've ever taken a Percocet then you've taken oxycodone. The only difference is that a Percocet usually has between five and seven and a half milligrams of it. Taking a Roxy is like taking six Percocets without any of the Acetaminophen. They are really strong, is what I'm trying to say.

Florida, God bless it, doesn't regulate how many pain pills you can get. The doctor gave me a script for two hundred and fifty Roxies. I can sell each one for fifteen bucks if I wanted to, but I'm not interested in selling.

The pill-mills have their own pharmacy but I go to a Walgreens by my apartment. The pill-mill pharmacies aren't accustomed to serving people with insurance or people who aren't paying in cash, plus if I get the pills there I'll have to deal with all of the people in the parking lot trying to hit me up.

Even at the Walgreens by my apartment there are people who loiter outside trying to buy pills from people as they walk out but not as bad as the pill-mill. You see them everywhere in Florida. Go to any pharmacy and you will see suspicious people just sitting in their cars smoking cigarettes, waiting. That's why you don't go at night. If they can't buy the drugs, they will take them. And they will hurt you to get them if they have to.

It's almost dark now. I take the pills and leave, passing a few people who try to make eye contact with me.

CHAPTER FOUR

I sit down at my desk and look at the bottle of pills. I've never seen this many before.

This could be bad.

This could be really bad.

Why do I feel so fucking happy then?

I guess if I get used to shooting these things up I won't have to steal from work anymore.

Yeah, this is a good thing. This could save my job. It could save me all the hassle of stealing while I'm at work and looking all over town for drugs when I'm off.

Yeah, this is a good thing.

I take six pills out of the bottle and put them in a cellophane baggie to give to Tom. I'm sure I owe him at least six.

I walk over to his apartment and see Bobby's moped parked out front. The light is on inside.

Bobby is in his early twenties. I think he just turned twenty-one, actually. He seems to effortlessly be able to go on and come off drugs whenever he wants. Sometimes he has them, sometimes he doesn't, either way he's in a good mood. It's refreshing to be around someone like him. He lives with his parents here on Davis Island and I think he does some kind of construction work with his father and collects unemployment between jobs. He never seems hard up for money and is always down to party. I'm not sure how he and Tom became so close but it's kind of sweet seeing them together. They compliment each other well.

I knock on the door. I can hear Tom singing a Michael Jackson song in a high-pitched voice on the other side. He stops singing and opens the door. No shirt again. Judging by the size of his smile and the sweat on his round belly I can tell he's been drinking and snorting pills. Bobby is standing in the kitchenette eating a ham sandwich with a grin on his face.

"Jack! What the fuck, bro, come on in. You want a Percocet? Beer?"

"I'll take a beer. Here you go," I say, as I hand him the pills.

He gives me a big, sweaty hug.

"What's that, Uncle Tom?" asks Bobby from the kitchen.

"Our male nurse friend Jack here just brought us some Roxy's."

"Fuck yeah! Let's crush one up!"

Tom sits down on his futon and crushes up one of the pills on a plate and then arranges three big, clumpy lines with a credit card. He hands me a rolled up dollar and I inhale mine and then chase it with warm beer. I can taste the chemicals running down the back of my throat. I've grown to love that bitter taste.

After we snort our lines and drink another beer, Bobby suggests we all go down to the beach. Davis Island is, well, an island after all, and there is a nice little dog beach down the street that we often go to.

I tell them that I have to go to my apartment to take a shit before we leave. Opiate addicts are sympathetic when it comes to shits because they are so rare for us. Tom reminds me to bring my guitar as I walk out.

I walk into my apartment and make sure that my blinds are all closed. Godzilla has damaged some of them from barking at neighbors and scratching at the windows so it takes some finagling to get them just right so no one can see inside.

Godzilla watches me as I crush up half a pill on my desk and scoop the powder into a bottle cap.

I open my desk drawer and pull out a pair of pliers and an insulin syringe.

I've only done this a few times.

I drip a small amount of water into the bottle cap.

I rip a filter off of one of my cigarettes, remove the paper, and then cut it in half.

I hold up the bottle cap with the pliers and then hold a flame up to the bottom of the cap until the water starts to bubble.

I drop the filter into the solution and it expands with the liquid.

I stick the needle into the filter and pull back the plunger to extract all of the liquid.

I swallow the filter like a pill so as not to waste anything.

I don't even need a tourniquet with these tiny needles but I use the ACE bandage anyways.

I shoot up the pill and it feels like Dilaudid, only not as clean. It doesn't give me that sterile, metallic taste, but the overall sense of connection and oneness is there.

I look down and Godzilla is staring at me with his tongue sticking out. I attach a leash to his collar and grab my guitar then go and get Tom and Bobby.

We all load up into my car and drive to the dog beach where we sing songs, drink, and snort pills until the sun comes up.

CHAPTER FIVE

I wake up at noon to the sound of my phone ringing. Godzilla is passed out by my head. His paws and belly are still wet and covered in sand. I sit up and realize that the whole couch is covered in sand and that it's made it's way into every crevice of my body.

It's the hospital calling. This could be bad.

There is a part of me that knows that what I'm doing can't and won't last forever. Eventually someone is going to catch on. Somehow I always manage to convince myself that I'm ahead of the game, though. *I've got this*, I tell myself.

It could be my boss calling me to ask me if I want to pick up a shift. I'm always the first person they call because I'm always willing to come in on my days off because I'm always hard up for drugs and money. Not today, though. The bottle of pills is sitting beside my phone on the coffee table and just looking at it sets my mind at ease.

No matter what happens, I've got the drugs, I'm going to be okay.

Having this many pills gives someone like me a sense of freedom. I don't need anyone or anything right now. If they ask me to come in, I will politely say no and then shoot up and feel good about myself.

I answer the phone and light a cigarette simultaneously.
"Hello?"

"Jack. Hey, it's me, Amy."

Amy, Amy, Amy... Oh yeah, Amy. The pharmacist. Shit. Amy is the pharmacist who oversees our floor. She has an office by the break room where she reviews all of the doctors' orders and makes sure that they are all put into the computer correctly. She's quiet. Thick glasses. Thick legs. Doesn't wear make up. Nice, natural rack. I fucked her once while I was still working the day shift and haven't really spoken to her since. I think she was turned off by how "drunk" I got when we hooked up. She's way too smart to get hung up on a guy like me.

"Oh, hey, Amy. What's up?"

"I need you to come to the hospital. I need to talk to you."

"Look, if it's about that night, I—"

"This has nothing to do with what happened. That was a mistake. This has to do with your job. Come in right now and come straight to my office."

She hung up. I guess I don't have much of a choice.

This is bad. It has to be bad.

I swallow a Roxy and snort a half of another one and then take Godzilla out for a walk. No time for a shower.

I chain-smoke as I drive to the hospital and drink rum and coke from my coffee cup and pray that no one will smell it on my breath.

I pull into the parking garage. I'm not used to seeing it in the full-on daylight. The building looks so bright that it hurts my eyes. The humidity is unbearable. I don't know how the day people do it.

I walk through the halls carrying my badge in my hand.

I see a few nurses and PCT's that I used to work with on the day shift and they wave as I pass.

I get to my floor and walk to Amy's office without anyone seeing me. She stands up from her desk and closes the door behind me.

"You have to quit, Jack."

"Quit? What are you talking about?"

She hands me a line graph with all of the nurse's names on it.

"This graph illustrates how much Dilaudid and Morphine nurses pull from the Pyxis. Do you see where your name is on this chart? Way over there to the right? You pulled more than three times the amount of Dilaudid as the average nurse on this floor last month."

"Yeah, that's because I work a lot. And I always take the difficult patients. This doesn't mean anything."

"I looked at a few of your patients' charts, Jack. I looked at how many times you pulled drugs versus how many times you signed them out. I don't have to tell you how many discrepancies I found."

"I'm busy, Amy. I don't always have time so sign everything out."

"Jack. I called you in here to tell you that I have to submit these reports. After I do, people are going to start looking into your charts and they are going to find the same things that I found. There is a chance that they will call the police, Jack. The amount that you have taken, it looks like you're selling it. There is no way a person can use this much themselves."

She has no idea.

"If they approach me, I'll just explain myself. I'm not stealing any drugs."

"If you quit, they might not even bother looking into it. Maybe they'll just let you go and that will be it. That is your best option right now."

"But I—"

"Quit, Jack. Go tell your boss that you have to leave and that you're not coming back. Enough with the bullshit."

"Okay."

Fuck.

My boss's office is a little further down the hall. Her door is closed but I can see that the light is on. I know she's in there. What am I going to say?

I walk to her door. Shit.

A few nurses walk by and try to make small talk but I'm too distracted.

I knock on the door and she tells me to come in.

"Mrs. Price. Stacey. Umm…"

"Jack, so good to see you. I never get to see you now that you work nights. We miss you, hun."

She is bright and sunny. Very southern.

"Stacy, I have to leave."

"What do you mean?"

"Family issues. I have some family things that I have to do. I, I can't work here anymore. I'm sorry."

"I'm sorry to hear that, Jack. You know people normally put in a two weeks notice so we have time to find a replacement. That's the way this usually works."

"I know. I'm sorry. Something just came up and I have to leave today."

She walks over and gives me a hug. She wears way too much perfume but right now I don't mind.

"Jack, you've always been a good employee here. I always hear good things about you from patients. If it was someone else I would be upset about you leaving like this, but I know that it must be something important for you to quit on us."

"It is, Stacey. Thank you for understanding."

"Is there anything I can do to help? You know you'll always have a job here if you want one."

"No. Nothing. Thanks again."

I hand her my badge and walk out of her office. I pass by Amy on my way out and we make a brief eye contact and I nod as if to say thank you. Her thick legs are crossed and she's wearing a skirt and now I wish that I had fucked her more than once.

What am I going to do? I need my job. I need my Dilaudid. I need my insurance. I need my money. What the hell am I going to do?

I pull over at a gas station. I crush up a pill and snort it before I go inside and get a big Heineken.

I can't get rid of the anxiety. Who can I call? I need to talk to someone. Myka. I need to call Myka. After I get home I'll call Myka and see if I can stop by her apartment.

I pull onto the only road that leads to Davis Island. My island. I don't want to face my apartment. I don't want to face Godzilla, my best buddy. I'm ashamed.

I see police cars with their sirens on in front of my complex.

Oh my God, they're here for me. This is it.

I slow down. There is an ambulance. This makes me feel better.

I see Bobby's moped parked in front of the complex.

Bobby is standing by Tom's apartment talking to police officers.

The parking lot is blocked so I have to park on the road.

I get out of my car and run up to Bobby, who is still talking to the police.

He turns and hugs me as I approach. I look at the cops as Bobby clings to me crying.

I look at Tom's apartment and see two paramedics wheeling a stretcher toward the ambulance with a body on top wrapped in a black bag. I see the unmistakable round belly.

"What happened, Bobby?"

"Tom, man. Fuckin' asshole took too much. I got to his apartment and the fat asshole was dead in his chair."

PART 2

CHAPTER SIX

His eyes looked yellow. The way the air looks yellow just before a summer storm. I don't think he blinked once the whole time I was outside. Above his right eye, the bottom half of a syringe was tattooed, and below the eye was the top half. The needle came all the way down to the edge of his razor sharp jaw. The edges of his buzz-cut hair were clean and straight. Tattooed below his left eye was the number 813, which must have been in reference to our area code. Across the front of his thick, sweaty neck was the word Zeus. The Z and the S were jagged and looked like mirror images of each other. They were placed below each ear. The E and the U were smaller and were placed on each side of his trachea.

As I was walking Godzilla I saw this man leaning against a black BMW parked on the road. He stared at me the whole time. He was huge. Not ripped huge, like a body builder, more like prison huge. Bulky and solid. A good, dense blend of muscle and fat. His shoulders were rounded and hunched over. His arms were thick and his hands looked like heavy chunks of tattooed meat.

Why was he watching me? Who the fuck was that guy?

I walk into my apartment and take off Godzilla's leash. I give him a dog treat then walk over to my window to see if I can see him.

I can see his car but he's not there.

Where the hell is he?

Bang! Bang! Bang! Bang!

Jesus Christ!

The knock on my door is so loud and hard that it shakes the walls of my apartment. Godzilla is barking with so much intensity that he's hopping off the ground with each yelp.

What should I do? Should I call the police? I know it's him.

I wait.

Maybe he'll just go away.

What am I talking about, he knows I'm in here. Who the fuck is he?

I think back to all the girls that I've hooked up with at the hospital. There is a good chance that I slept with this man's girlfriend. Or wife! Jesus Christ he's going to kill me.

"Open up, bruh! Right now! I seen you in there, boi, open the fuckin' door!"

His voice sounds like a raspy bark. Like there's broken glass in his throat.

I look at my desk and there are two fat, blue lines of powder on an old nursing textbook. I bend down and snort both of them in one inhalation.

I open the door.

"Damn, bruh, what the fuck took you so long. You heard me knockin'. You seen me standin' there."

"Sorry, man, it's just, I don't know you, and I wasn't sure what, I mean, I didn't know if you—"

"You a male nurse?"

"A male nurse? Uh, yeah, I'm a nurse. I'm male."

"You gay?"

"Um, no, I'm not gay. What are you—?"

"You get a lot of pussy?"

"Um… Yeah, sometimes."

"I know a dude who works in a hospital. He ain't no nurse or nothin' but he gets hella pussy."

"I'm sorry, what's your name?"

"Zeus, bruh. Look at my damn neck."

"Do I know you?"

"Nah, nigga we don't know each other. I was sent here to get yo ass."

"Get me?"

"Pick you up, bruh. We gonna go for a ride, me and you."

"Where are we going?"

"Don't matter. What matters is that you get in the damn car."

"I can't. I have things to do today. I mean, I just lost my job, and—"

"I wasn't askin' you. I'm tellin' you, you comin' with me. We can do this easy or hard, don't make no difference to me. You gettin' in the car either way."

"Who sent you here to get me?"

"That don't matter neither. All that matters right now is that you get in that car. You do that and we cool."

I guess that about settles it.

I grab my cigarettes, my wallet, and a couple pills and then follow Zeus out to his car. He walks around to the driver's side and looks at me as I stand by the passenger door. He knows that I don't want to get in and he seems amused by it.

"What the fuck you waitin' for? You want me to open the door for you, homie? Come on, get the fuck in."

I open the door and sit down in the passenger seat. It's dark inside the car. The windows are tinted to the point that I can barely see out. There is a paper cup in the cup holder filled with blunt roaches. He catches me staring at the roaches and I see him smile for the first time. All of his teeth, top and bottom, are silver. Shiny, glistening silver. Maybe platinum. I've heard of people getting platinum grills and I've seen a few on TV but never in real life. They're really quite extraordinary.

"You smoke, bruh?"

"Sometimes. I stick to pills mostly. I have a bad hip."

"I bet you do, homie. I bet you fuckin' do."

He starts the engine and bites his bottom lip as he slams his foot down on the gas pedal. The tires burn out as we make an illegal U-turn and leave the island.

What the hell is going on?

CHAPTER SEVEN

We pull into a parking lot after a short drive. The concrete lot surrounds a plain, rectangular, brick building. Beyond the parking lot I can see marshland. I can smell the mud through the windows. Must be low tide.

"Where are we?" I ask timidly.

"New Beginnings, nigga. This a rehab clinic."

"You're taking me to a rehab clinic? What the fuck, man? Someone sent you here to check me into a rehab?"

"Nah, bruh," he says through a raspy giggle. "You here to work. You just like me now. You gonna work for these fools."

"I'm confused. I think maybe you have the wrong person or something. I didn't apply for any job at any rehab clinic, or anywhere. I just quit my job yesterday."

"Come on inside, playa. They gonna tell you everything. You gonna see Mr. Braxton, the manager. He waitin' for you, bruh. Come on."

I follow Zeus across the parking lot. As confused and scared as I am I can't stop thinking about his excessive use of the word "nigga". I mean, he looks like he probably has some Latino blood but he's definitely not black. I think we're getting a little too liberal about who can get away with saying that word.

I light a cigarette and Zeus snatches it out of my mouth and throws it on the ground in one quick motion.

"No smokin' inside, bruh. Come on."

I was actually going to smoke it before going in, but whatever. Asshole.

We walk inside and the air conditioner feels nice on my skin. The floors are covered in a short, brown carpet and the walls are yellow-tinged white.

Zeus talks to a young, black girl at the front desk. It's obvious that he's fucked her and wants to fuck her again. She pretends to be annoyed by him while giving him "fuck me" glances.

They stop talking and she stretches her neck out and looks around him to get a better look at me. She giggles and then he giggles.

What the hell is going on?

A big, brown, metal door swings open and a petite blonde girl in scrubs walks out. I can tell by her features that her hair is dyed blonde. She looks European. Italian, or Spanish maybe. She's wearing a nametag that says "Carrie B. RN"

"Here you go, Care Bear," says Zeus, as he looks her up and down. He bites his tattooed knuckles and leans back to looks at her round ass.

"Thanks, asshole. Come on back, uh, Jack is it?"

"Yeah, Jack. Jack Lawrence."

"Hi, Jack, I'm Carrie, Carrie Buck," she says, mocking my James Bondish response.

"What is this place? I mean, I know it's a rehab, but why—?"

"Save your questions, Jack. Just follow me."

I follow Carrie into a bright hallway and the door closes slowly behind us.

We walk down several long hallways and I see patients dressed in regular clothes. I do notice that no one has shoelaces or belts, though. I always imagined rehabs being louder. I expected to hear people screaming from the rooms as they withdrawal from drugs. The people here seem pretty complacent. Bored, actually.

It doesn't look like a bad place to work. Maybe a little slow for my taste, but it looks easy.

I ask if I can go to the restroom after I see a men's room by a nurse's station. Carrie sighs like I just asked her for a kidney.

I go inside the restroom and crush up half a pill on the back of the toilet with my driver's license. I snort it with a dollar then swallow the other half with a handful of water from the faucet.

At the end of a long, grey hallway, that looks like it's under maintenance, we come to a service elevator.

Carrie pulls out a key and sticks it in a keyhole by the up and down buttons. She turns the key and the buttons light up. She presses the down button and the doors open immediately with a loud ding.

We stand in the elevator and she is standing one step in front of me. She does have a really nice ass. Not "huge" like Jessica's but big enough to catch my attention. Her scrubs are all black and her hair is tied up in a red ribbon that matches her red and black tennis shoes. Her neck is long and smooth. I imagine pressing my lips just below her ear and kissing her skin. I imagine the sexy grin she would have on her face as I grab her hips from behind and pull her body close to mine.

Ding! The elevator door opens. We're now in the basement.

We walk down another long hallway with grey carpet on the floor. There are a few pictures hanging on the walls that look like someone chose without too much consideration. Like they were bought randomly just to occupy wall space.

Carrie walks a few steps ahead of me. She gets to a wooden door and stops. She knocks gently and a voice on the other side tells her to come in. She opens the door.

There is a man sitting behind a desk talking on the phone. There are no windows or pictures on the walls. The man looks up at me and motions for me to sit down. I turn and look at Carrie and she walks out without saying goodbye. I sit down on the hard chair and wait for the man to finish his phone call.

The man is chubby and his hair is orange. He looks uncomfortable in his own skin. His clothes are too small. He looks swollen. Probably too much salt in his diet.

He hangs up the phone then stands up and reaches over his desk to shake my hand.

"Jack Lawrence. Good to meet you, my name is Hugh Braxton, I'm the manager of the Bright Futures division here at New Beginnings."

"Nice to meet you, Hugh. Can you please tell me why I'm here? And why a man who looks like he belongs in a chain-gang brought me here?"

"Work, Jack. You're going to work here."

"Is that so? What the hell kind of a place is this? What makes you think I would have any interest in working here? You think you can intimidate me into working here by sending some thug to pick me up? Fuck you!"

"Calm down, Jack. We don't need to use Zeus to intimidate you. You are going to work for us either way and I'll tell you why."

"What the fuck are you—?"

"Listen!" he shouts. The room gets very quiet. "You are going to work for us because we know everything there is to know about you. We know where you're from, we know about your family, your ex-girlfriend, and most importantly, we know what you've done. We know everything that you've done. The stealing of drugs, the using of drugs, the distribution of drugs, oh, and most recently, we know that you gave drugs to a man who died after taking them. A man who comes from a very wealthy family that would love to get their hands you."

"Who are you? What the hell is this?"

"This is what we do, Jack. Everyone who works here in the Bright Future division is just like you. They all have secrets that we know. And we keep your secrets, Jack, don't worry. All we ask in return for *our* silence, is *your* silence. You will not speak of any of the things that we do here in the Bright Futures division or we will let the police know the things that we know. We will show them the mounds of evidence that we have collected on you, Jack. And if you give us any trouble, well, you met Zeus. He doesn't have much of a conscious, Jack. He's been working for us for some time now and he's never let us down. Are we clear?"

"Are we clear? Are you fucking kidding me? You're blackmailing me into working for you? What the hell kind of place is this?"

"We need people like you, Jack. We need smart people with secrets. People who are good at what they do but not necessarily good at making life decisions, if that makes sense. That is how we have maintained our anonymity all these years."

"Why me, though? Why a nurse? What do you need a nurse for?"

"We do some procedures here. Very small procedures, nothing too complicated. We have a full medical staff."

"And they're all like me? Addicts?"

"Drug addicts, criminals, murderers even."

"Murderers?"

"You would be surprised, Jack. With the amount of money that we have at our disposal we can pretty much make anything go away. As long as you're with us, you're safe. You don't have to worry about the police ever finding out about any of the things that you've done. And if they do, we can make them all go away. Trust me."

"So, what is it exactly that I would be doing?"

"It's just like any other nursing job, Jack. You come in, you get your assignment, you care for you patients, you act as the doctor's eyes and ears, and then you go home at the end of the day. A free man."

"What kind of procedures are we talking about here?"

"We'll get into that after you start your training. I assure you there is nothing here that you can't handle. Oh, and don't worry about the drugs. What you do on your time is your business not ours."

"When do I start?"

"You're going to come in tomorrow to start your training. Zeus will drive you back home now. Do you remember how to get here?"

"Yeah, I think so."

"Good. Be here at 9 a.m. and we'll get you started."

He pushes a button on his phone and a woman on an intercom answers. He tells her to send Carrie back down to walk me out.

I try to make conversation with Carrie as we walk down the hallway and ride in the elevator but she doesn't seem interested.

I have so many questions.

I wonder what she did to end up here? She doesn't look like an addict.

We get to the lobby and Zeus is still leaning against the front counter flirting with the receptionist. He says goodbye and tells her that he's going to call her later tonight but the promise sounds empty.

The sun hits my face like a Mack truck as I walk outside and light a cigarette. Blinding, white hot Florida heat.

"You ain't gonna smoke that in my car, bruh."

"What? You have, like, a thousand roaches in your car."

"Damn straight. You wanna smoke weed, that's cool, no cigarettes, though. That shit is nasty."

I take long, deep drags as we walk to his car and then drop the cigarette on the concrete and step on it before getting in.

He sprays cologne into the air after he closes the door and starts the ignition.

"That shit stank, bruh."

"Whatever, man. I need to get home."

He turns his music up so loud that it literally hurts my head. Each beat feels like a punch in the back of the neck. I look over at him and I can see all of his silver teeth shining in the sun as he smiles and raps along to the song.

I try my best to scream over the music.

"How long have you worked there?"

"What?"

"I said, how long have you worked there? Can you turn it down?"

He turns it down with an angry look on his face.

"I been workin' for them niggas a while, bruh. They got shit on me and they got shit on my daughter's mother. I don't work for them, we both go to jail and my baby girl probably end up in foster care."

"Shit. That sucks."

"Ain't all bad, bruh. I ain't gotta worry about the police fuckin' with me no more. I sell my shit, I do my thang, them niggas got the police in they pocket. They own the police. Long as I keep doin' what they ask me to do, I'm good. My daughter's good."

"So, you sell drugs, too?"

"Shit, bruh, I gotta sell drugs at this point. Look at me. Who you think gonna hire me? I done time. I done years, bruh, and not just for drug shit either, for violent shit. But that's my life. That's the life I was born into. Violence isn't somethin' I chose, homie. Violence is somethin' I learned to survive. I'm a product of the way I was raised, my surroundings. You think I chose this? Nah, bruh, I just as well be like one of you niggas. Work a regular job, pay my bills, go to bed at night not worryin' about gettin' murdered in my sleep. These fools got me after I was about to go down for a murder charge along with some drug trafficking bullshit. They showed me a file they had on me and my baby's mama. Shit was big, bruh. I ain't gonna lie, I was scared. But they let me go. All I gotta do is bust some heads every now and again and everything's cool. For someone like me it's a pretty good option, ya heard?"

"Damn. So how did you get the name Zeus if you don't mind me asking?"

"My name's Jesus. My momma used to yell out my name when I was playin' on the block and the kids thought she was sayin' 'Hey Zeus' instead of Jesus. Just kinda stuck, I guess."

"Do you know what they do there? At the clinic."

"Ima let them explain it to you."

He drops me off at the front of my apartment and hands me a piece of paper with his phone number on it. He tells me to call him if I need anything. I assume he means drugs.

CHAPTER EIGHT

I walk into my apartment and sit down on my couch. It's still covered in sand. Godzilla pounces on my lap and licks my face as I stare blankly at a black TV screen. My phone is buzzing in my pocket. It's Jessica. I can't deal with that right now. She probably heard that I quit.

I sit at my desk and crush up a Roxy.

I cook it up, draw it up into a syringe, and inject it into a vein in my left wrist.

No relief.

The needle on the insulin syringe is too small to spray blood on my canvas.

Oh well.

I grab a beer and take Godzilla out for a walk.

I call Myka when I get outside.

I'm carrying a leash and a beer in my left hand, and a cigarette and a phone in my right hand.

"Myka. Hey, what's up?"

"Jack, what the fuck, man? You quit? I heard you quit."

"I had to. Something came up. What are you doing this evening?"

"I'm off tomorrow so I was planning on going out. Why the hell did you quit?"

"Let's meet up at Hooligan's. I'll buy you a beer."

"What time?"

"Seven or so?"

"Okay, I'll be there. Is everything okay, Jack?"

"Yeah, I'm fine. I'll see you at seven."

I go back into my apartment. I need to clean this shithole and take a shower. That'll make me feel better. But first I should probably check out Michelle on Facebook.

I log in and go straight to her page.

One new picture. It's her and him. They're smiling again. Arms wrapped around each other standing in some sunny field. Kids are playing in the background, flying kites. Oh shit, is that…? Yes it is. A fucking ring. I zoom the picture in on her hand and can see a shiny, gold ring on her ring finger. Why? Why him?

I close my laptop and try to get the image out of my head.

She can't get married.

In the back of my mind I still have this hope that one day I'll get clean and we'll end up back together and all this will be some lousy part of our past that we laugh about. An engagement makes it real. If they get married, my fantasy dies. I need that glimmer of hope. That's what keeps me going.

What if she gets pregnant?

I crush up and snort an Adderall, swallow another Roxy, crack open a beer, light a cigarette, turn on some music, and then begin to clean.

With all these distractions I still find myself thinking about her.

I think about her touch. That's what I miss the most. The way her fingers felt on my skin. All the Dilaudid in the world wouldn't feel as good as her touch. I think that's the feeling that I'm subconsciously trying to re-create with all these drugs. I'm trying to find the right combination that will make me feel as good as her tiny little fingers did, but nothing comes close.

Ok. Enough. I have bigger things to worry about. Like the fact that I am being blackmailed into working for a secret organization. That's what I should be worried about.

I clean the apartment with a compulsive intensity. I move all of the furniture and vacuum, then sweep, then mop. I open all the windows to air out the smell of smoke and dried up Godzilla piss. By the time I'm done the place looks nice. I've only seen it this clean a few times. I take a long shower and clean myself with the same attention to detail. After I get out, I lie down on the couch in my underwear and take a nice nap with the fresh air blowing through the window.

I wake up and it's 6:45. I throw on my clothes, take Godzilla out, pop a few pills, and then drive to Hooligan's to meet up with Myka.

Hooligan's is the first bar you get to after coming off Davis Island. It has a thatched roof and a large outdoor area with picnic tables and umbrellas. There is usually a Celtic band playing inside.

I park on the road.

I see Myka sitting at one of the picnic tables as I approach the building. She has a full pitcher of dark amber beer in front of her and two frosty glasses. The color of the beer makes me think about dehydration and urinary tract infections and it makes me miss the hospital.

"Myka! What's up?" I say, as she stands up and gives me a hug.

"What's up? You tell me what's up."

She looks me dead in the eye. She's a tough girl. Small and skinny, but intimidating somehow.

"I quit. I went and saw Stacy yesterday and told her that I couldn't work there anymore."

"I know, Jack. Why?"

I fill up one of the glasses and drink half of it then light a cigarette.

"I don't know, Myka. It's embarrassing."

"What? Just tell me."

"I got myself a little mixed up. With drugs."

"So? We all take drugs, we all drink, that's no reason to quit."

"I got really mixed up, though. I was stealing them."

"Shit, man. What the fuck? Are you fucking stupid?"

"Yeah. Amy called me and told me that she knew all about it and told me to quit before everyone else catches on."

"The pharmacist Amy? Didn't you fuck her?"

"Yeah."

"You're an asshole. You know that right?"

"I know."

"So what are you going to do now?"

"I'm going to work for a rehab place. New Beginnings."

"Rehab? Why the hell would you want to do that?"

"I don't know, Myka. I don't have a lot of options right now."

We sip our beers and Myka takes a few drags off my cigarette. I feel like she just lost a lot of respect for me. I have a real knack for letting people down. That's what happened with Michelle.

Michelle thought that I was going to give her the life that she always wanted. She saw such a bright future in my eyes. It killed me to see how optimistic she was and I never really understood why until now. It was because I always knew deep down inside that I was a scumbag. This depraved life that I have created for myself was always in the cards.

"Jack."

"What?"

I look up and Myka is staring past my face at something behind me.

"That girl over there is checking you out. She's hot. Wow. She looks like a ballerina. Like a Spanish, maybe South American, ballerina with a leather jacket on. Look back when you get a chance. She's the one with the dyed blonde hair. Crazy hot."

I refill my glass and casually turn around to see who she's talking about.

It's her, Carrie, the girl from New Beginnings.

I make eye contact with her and she motions for me to come towards her.

I tell Myka that I'll be right back and stand up.

Myka calls me an asshole again then goes inside to get more beer.

I approach Carrie and she grabs me by the hand and quickly leads me to the parking lot without a word.

She walks me to a sleek, black and red motorcycle and hands me a helmet.

"What? You want me to…"

She gets on the motorcycle and starts it up.

I climb onto the back and wrap my arms around her.

The engine whines as she twists the throttle with reckless abandon.

CHAPTER NINE

After a long, placid ride across the causeway we get to St. Pete beach. She parks the motorcycle in a motel parking lot and for a second I think she might have gotten a room for us. I'm excited.

"What are we doing? Do you have a room here?"

"Fuck no. Come on, let's go."

"What about your motorcycle? You're just going to leave it here?"

"I know the guy who runs this place. He doesn't mind. Come on."

I follow her across the street and we walk between two hotels to get to the beach.

We step onto the sand at the same time.

She stops.

I stop.

I think that she's just admiring the waves in the moonlight but I look over and she's taking off her clothes.

Best night ever.

"What are you—?"

"Just take off your clothes. Come on. We're getting in."

"In the ocean? What?"

She takes off everything but her underwear, lays everything out on the sand, and then wraps everything up in a nice bundle. I can see her body in the light from the hotel. She's flawless. Her tits have that wonderful natural jiggle as she moves around bundling up her things. Her ass has the same jiggle as she stands up and looks at me. I stare at her hips. They come out of her waist at almost a ninety-degree angle. They look so soft and inviting. It's so hard not to put my hands around her waist. I want to lift her up and feel those thick legs wrap around me and those tits rub up against my chest.

Shit. She's staring at me, staring at her, and she doesn't look amused.

I take off my clothes until I'm down to my boxers.

I wrap everything up the same way she did then we both walk to the water's edge and put our things in the sand.

"So, you just decided that you wanted to go for a swim?"

She runs full speed into the water and dives into a black wave. She disappears for a few seconds then I see her resurface a little further out.

The water touches my toes and it's cold.

I'm reluctant to jump.

She stands up and the water is only waist deep. I see her wet, slippery body glistening.

I run full speed and jump in.

I swim out to her and we both crouch down so that the water comes up to our necks. We bounce up and down with the swells. She puts her face right in front of mine. Her eyeliner is running and her hair is slicked back.

"This is the only place we can talk, Jack."

"What? What do you mean?"

"They're everywhere. I don't know how they do it, but they know everything. They hear everything."

"You mean, the people we work for?"

"Exactly. This is the only place that I feel safe talking."

"Jesus. This just keeps getting weirder."

"Tell me about it. I've been working there for over a year now."

"So how did you end up there?"

"It doesn't matter. What matters is that you don't talk about them. Never talk about any of the things that they do. They are dangerous, Jack. If you tell someone, they won't go after you, they will kill whoever you told. They are ruthless. I learned the hard way. That's why I wanted to find you early, before you had the chance to tell anyone."

"I don't even know what it is they do, though. I don't have anything to tell."

"Good."

"So, what do they do?"

"Do you know anything about eugenics?"

"Not really. Sounds familiar. Was that something Hitler was into or something?"

"We sterilize people. We take drug addicts, convicts, people with disabilities, pretty much anyone who needs financial or legal help who they don't think should procreate, and we sterilize them. We take away their ability to reproduce."

"What the fuck?"

"Yeah. I'm sure you've seen how these people can make things disappear right? They do the same thing for their 'clients'. They get them out of whatever trouble they've gotten themselves into, financial or legal, and in return they take away their ability to have children."

"Who's behind all of this? They must have a lot of money to keep something like this going."

"I don't know all of the people involved but I do know that the Goodell family is one of the major contributors. They might have actually started the whole thing. I think pretty much all of the wealthy families in Tampa contribute in one way or another."

"How long has this been going on?"

"I'm not sure. I know it's been over thirty years."

"How do you know that?"

"They'll explain it to you tomorrow on your first day. They have a bunch of statistics compiled that show that what they are doing has actually decreased the crime rate and made Tampa safer. It's all bullshit."

"I can't believe this. You can't take away someone's ability to have children. Can you? I mean, that's what this is all about right? Life? Biologically, it's our purpose, it's what we're designed to do."

"It doesn't matter what you believe, Jack. You better come to terms with it fast because you are a part of it now whether you like it or not. There is no way out. For all intents and purposes, you belong to them."

"This is bullshit. You know, my neighbor was a Goodell. His name was Tom. I gave him some pills the other night and a friend of ours found him dead the next morning from taking them. That's what they've got on me. One of the things they've got on me."

"That's probably not a coincidence, Jack."

"Yeah, something's not right about all this. Are you going to tell me how you ended up there?"

"No."

"Okay."

"Let's go. I need to get you home. You need a good night's sleep. Tomorrow's your first day."

"Great."

We walk out of the water. I let her walk a few steps ahead of me so I can watch her wet ass and thighs move as she walks through the sand.

We put our clothes on and walk back to her motorcycle.

We once again fly over the causeway in the silent isolation of our helmets. The wind dries our skin and clothes leaving behind a thin layer of salt and sand.

I get home and call Myka to apologize for leaving her. She calls me an asshole again but tells me that she understands and that she would have done the same thing with a girl as hot as her.

I shoot up and take Godzilla out for a walk. It's a beautiful night. Muggy and warm, but beautiful. Storm clouds are flowing across the moon too fast to let any rain fall.

I take an Ambien and a Klonopin then get comfortable on the couch with Godzilla.

CHAPTER TEN

I'm not going in. I'm just going to stay here on the couch. I'm not getting up. Fuck them. Fuck the clinic, fuck whatever dirt they have on me, fuck it all. I don't care. I'm staying in bed.

I turn off my alarm, roll over, and go back to sleep.

Godzilla is barking. Goddamn blinds must be open. I don't want to open my eyes. I just want to stay here on my couch with the blanket pulled over my head. I think enviously about all of my old, bedridden patients lying in their hospital beds with morphine being slowly fed into their veins while people turn their bodies and clean them. Just slipping away into some euphoric nothingness. I want that right now. I want an excuse to close my eyes and ignore the world.

I feel something on my shoulder.

Please God let it be Godzilla.

My blanket flies off my body and I feel the cold air from my air conditioner on my sweaty skin.

I flop over and a hand grabs me by the throat and pins me onto the couch.

It's him, Zeus. He's smiling. I see his silver teeth close up for the first time. They look clean and kind of beautiful.

Godzilla is barking and scratching Zeus' legs but he doesn't seem to notice.

"I was hoping I would get some company today, Man Nurse."

"What the fuck are you doing in my apartment? How did you get in?"

"Never mind that. Get your clothes on, bruh, you comin' with me on a job."

"A job? Why the hell—?"

"Get the fuck up!"

I jump off the couch and grab my pants. He steps up close to me and flexes his shoulder muscles. He's the most intimidating person I've ever seen. He smiles. I continue getting dressed.

After I put my clothes on I tell him that I have to take Godzilla out.

He sits down at my desk and pours two Roxies out of my prescription bottle and starts crushing them up on a book with the handle of a knife.

"Go on then. Make it quick. We ain't got a whole lot of time."

I walk back inside my apartment after walking Godzilla and he's still sitting at my desk. He was kind enough to leave me one fat line of blue powder. Probably three quarters of a pill's worth.

"Listen, Zeus, I don't want to be a part of any of this. I really don't. I think I'm just going to deal with the consequences of whatever I've done. If I go to jail, then so be it."

"You funny, bruh. You think you have a choice in the matter? I like you, bruh. Come on."

"Where are we going?"

"Boss man told me to bring you out on a job with me so you can see how we do things round here. So you know what you're dealin' with, should you decide to turn down his offer of employment. You gonna like this, homie."

We get into his car and he turns up his music so loud that it feels like the windows are going to shatter. He appears to be in a good mood. I thought that he was just being evil when he told me that he was glad to have some company but I'm starting to think that he was being genuine. He puffs on a blunt and nods his head as he raps along with the song that's playing. The more time I spend with this guy, the less nervous I feel around him.

We drive to a neighborhood near the Hillsborough River.

He turns the music down as we creep down the residential streets looking for a specific house.

His face turns from smiling and friendly to laser focused. Like a lion sneaking up on a herd of zebras.

I try to talk and he shushes me.

He taps out his blunt and rolls up the windows.

He shuts off the engine and gets out. I follow him.

He walks around to the trunk and presses a button on his keychain to pop it open then reaches in and pulls out a huge over-the-top machine gun. I think it's an AK-47 but I don't know much about guns and I don't want to ask him.

He nestles the gun up against his hip with his right hand on the handle and his finger on the trigger and starts walking toward the house. I follow close behind.

We get to the front door and he raises one of his heavy, black boots and kicks the door open. He points the gun to the ceiling and blasts off five rounds and I instinctually duck down and cover my head. The gun is much louder than I expected. I guess he's not too worried about making a scene.

"Jesse Gonzalez!" he screams as he fires off two more rounds into the ceiling. "Come on out mother fucker!"

I have no idea what's going on but I'm scared. My hands and knees are shaking.

Zeus's eyes are blank. He looks completely insane but completely calm and collected at the same time which makes him that much more scary.

A small man comes out of a bedroom begging Zeus to leave his family alone. His hands are in the air and he is speaking in half Spanish half English.

"Jack! Come on over here, boi. I want you to see this."

I walk over next to Zeus. The man in front of us is trembling almost as badly as I am.

"This man here broke a promise. Now, he knows damn well what the penalty is for breaking a promise but he chose to do it anyways. What's your opinion on the death penalty, Jack?"

"I don't know. I guess, I don't know, I can see how under some circumstances—"

"I'm against the death penalty, believe it or not. You see, you can't convince people that murder is wrong with the threat of murdering them. That shit's crazy. Basically, they sayin' murder is okay as long as the person you killin' meets their criteria to be killed. But the people out on the streets have they own criteria, know what I'm sayin'? The government says if you kill someone then you deserve to die. A man in the hood might say that if you fuck his wife you deserve to die. Or if you steal his drugs you deserve to die. The man in the hood and the government ain't so different. They both feel that there are lines that a man shouldn't cross lest he get himself killed. Now, like I said, I don't agree with it, but that's the way it is and it ain't gonna change any time soon. This man here made a deal and he didn't hold up his end of things. My boss believes that this is grounds for death, bruh."

"Zeus, you're not going to—"

Pop! Pop! Pop!

Three bullets smack into the man's chest and he flies back against the wall in the hallway. The white paint is sprayed red. It looks just like my canvas.

I hear crying in the bedroom. I don't even want to think about who is behind the door crying. It's a female voice and it sounds young.

I look down at the body and I think about the first time I saw a dead body in the hospital. I remember expecting to feel more. I approached the body and expected to be overwhelmed with emotion but I didn't feel anything. The skin looked like wax. Another nurse told me to wrap up the head to close the jaw so it didn't get stuck open. It was a body, not a person. I helped the nurses and PCTs move it and I remember the sound and the feel of the bones snapping in and out of their sockets without the muscle tension to hold them in place. I wheeled the body down to the basement by myself and put it in a cooler with a dozen or so other bodies.

The man bleeding on the floor in front of me is dying. My instincts as a nurse are telling me to help him but I can't. His eyes are closed. The room smells like smoke and blood. Zeus is staring at me with a terrible smile on his face. I think he kept his eyes on me throughout the whole thing, just enjoying watching my reaction to it all.

"Grab the feet, bruh."

"What?"

"Grab the fuckin' feet, brug, we gettin' outta here."

He wraps his right arm underneath the man's left arm and grips onto his shirt and I grab his feet. We lift the body and Zeus leads the way as we walk out to his car. Several neighbors are standing outside. Zeus makes eye contact with everyone staring at us and they all turn around and run back into their houses.

We toss the body into the trunk and Zeus closes the door. He throws his gun in the back seat and we get in and drive away with the music blaring.

I'm speechless. Zeus looks happy.

We drive to a nature preserve a few miles off Interstate 4. I know exactly where this is leading. I think I knew it the second we got into the car.

Zeus parks on the side of the road where there is a small concrete boat ramp that leads into a river. There are no other cars anywhere in sight.

"Gotta keep them gators fed, boi!"

"So, we're dropping the body here?"

"Nah, bruh, we just goin' for a swim."

Asshole.

I help him unload the body and drag it to the boat ramp. Zeus pulls a large knife out of his pocket and cuts all of the man's clothes off.

I look out onto the water and see several pairs of reptilian eyes peeking over the surface. They move toward us. Jesus, he must have these damn things trained.

"Ya see, Jack, the trick is, you gotta feed them gators, like, once or twice a week. They know me now. Look at 'em. Ya see how they come swimmin' up on me like that. They pretty much my pets, bruh. Them gators been raised on human meat. I been feedin' 'em since they was little."

He tosses the naked body into the water with one hand effortlessly, like he's tossing a bag of garbage.

The body floats out into the current face down. Thank God.

The alligators surround it and I turn away. I can hear thrashing. I look over at Zeus and he is watching with his big, silver grin. He lights a blunt and blows out a cloud of smoke. He watches like a proud father.

"Why did you bring me here, Zeus. This is too much, man."

"What do you mean why? You know damn well why I had to bring you out here. Look, bruh, you cool, I like you, but if you fuck around and they give me the order to toss your ass out here, I'll do it in a heartbeat. I won't even think twice, bruh. I got rid of plenty people I liked a lot more than you. At the end of the day, me and my family come first. And if I don't do what they say, my family gonna suffer. You decide to play games, not show up, try to run away, you gonna meet my AK, bruh. And I ain't gonna lose no sleep over it neither."

"You made your point. Can we go back now?"

"I'm gonna do you a favor cause I like you. I'm gonna tell the boss man that this whole thing took a lot longer than it did. You go home and get some rest. Then, you show up at work on time tomorrow or we gonna have to have another talk."

I take a pill out of my wallet and swallow it then light a cigarette.

Zeus hands me the clothes and tells me that it's my job to get rid of them then reminds me that I am now an accomplice to a murder, which is another thing they have on me.

We get into the car and drive back to Davis Island.

PART 3

CHAPTER ELEVEN

It's Friday morning. Seven o'clock. I'm up and getting dressed on autopilot. I'm having trouble adjusting to being a day person. I look outside and suddenly living in Florida doesn't make sense. Why would anyone choose this unrelenting sunshine and heat? How the hell did I end up here and why am I still here? Most of the people in this state are people who came here on vacation and decided that it was their life goal to live here. They worked hard and did what they needed to do then made the big move. The answer to all of their problems. At first it's nice. Sunshine every day. Warm, sandy beaches and palm trees. But one day they wake up and look out their window hoping for a cloudy day, praying for a break in the heat and humidity, and that day doesn't come. The sunshine bears down on them every second, of every, fucking, day. They realize that they are now trapped indoors more than they were when they were battling snowstorms up north. Suddenly the snow-storms don't seem so bad. In fact, they find themselves fantasizing about them. They find themselves fantasizing about grey, cold, rainy days, sitting inside and drinking coffee and reading a book. Those fantasies replace fantasies of sitting on beaches in the sun. The feel of the sun on their shoulders begins to feel like the unwanted touch of a stranger that makes you recoil in disgust.

Working nights, I had forgotten how miserable this place is.

I walk Godzilla and it's like I never took a shower. I'm drenched in a sweat that smells like a mixture of deodorant and the chemicals that leak out of my pores now.

Before I leave, I load up a syringe but decide not to shoot up at the last minute. I'm not sure why.

I snort half a pill and swallow the other half then put five more in a cellophane baggie to bring with me to work.

I climb into my car and the heat almost causes me to lose consciousness.

I stop by the gas station for some cigarettes and notice a familiar booming noise coming from the side of the building.

I peek around the corner and see Zeus sitting in his car nodding his head and rapping. He looks up at me and gives me an upward nod and a smile to let me know that he's okay with me knowing that he's following me.

I think back to the man that he shot and fed to the alligators. In a way I envy him. Whatever shit he had gotten himself into was over now. No more stress. No more looking over his shoulder. His game was over and mine was getting more and more complicated. More stressful and confusing.

I get back into my car and drive to New Beginnings.

I arrive at work and Carrie greets me at the door. I give her an unrequited smile. She acts like she has never seen me before and is annoyed by my attempt at friendliness. She hands me a badge and leads me through the big, brown door and I follow her to a conference room. As we walk, I see two nurses and one patient that I already want to fuck.

Carrie opens the door to the conference room and tells me to be seated. I sit down and she gives me an almost indiscernible smile when she catches me checking out her body. She's wearing white scrub pants and

I can clearly see a black thong underneath them. I didn't even try to act like I wasn't looking and when she caught me she didn't look annoyed or angry, which I take as a sign of better things to come.

"Someone will be with you shortly, Mr. Lawrence. In the meantime, watch this video."

She turns on a television with an old VCR attached to it. She pushes play on the VCR and the movie begins. Carrie walks out after giving me one more look that could easily be interpreted as a smile.

I find myself nodding off as the movie plays. It's a low budget documentary about the history of eugenics. I pull out my cellophane and pop a pill without any water. Just as I'm tucking it back into my pocket, Mr. Braxton opens the door and walks in. He turns off the television then shakes my hand and sits down beside me.

"What did you think of the film, Jack?"

"Pretty good. Informative."

"Cut the shit, Jack. That movie is terrible. We just play it when we need to buy time. It's very old and outdated. So, what do you know about eugenics? Anything?"

"Not much. It's when people decide who can and who can't reproduce, right? Weeding out the bad genes?"

"Pretty much. Do you agree with it, Jack?"

"Honestly, sir, I don't. Not that it really matters."

"No, it doesn't matter, but can I ask why it is that you don't agree with it?"

"It just seems cruel to take away people's ability to have children. From what I've heard, that's the greatest joy that us humans can experience. It's what millions of years of evolution has programmed us to do."

"Have you ever been to the children's hospital around the corner there, Jack?"

"Can't say that I have. I know a few nurses who work there, though."

"Let me show you a little video I put together on my phone."

I lean over Mr. Braxton's shoulder and look at his phone. He opens up a page with a video labeled "Children's Hospital" and pushes the play button.

"See these children, Jack?"

I look at the phone and see pictures of babies and toddlers born with physical deformities and obvious neurological disorders. I see nurses and physical therapists helping the children up out of bed and feeding them. Some of them receive their food through tubes going straight into their stomach, and some through tubes that snake down their noses and into their guts. The staff is cleaning the children and moving their contorted limbs to improve their range of motion. Several of the children have tracheotomies and the video shows staff cleaning the gaping holes in their necks. It's too much to watch. I actually had to leave the hospital during my pediatric rotation in nursing school because I couldn't handle it. I pretended to be sick so I didn't have to look at the poor children. I'm not proud of this, but it's true.

"What do you think the best treatment is for cancer? Or even AIDS?" Mr. Braxton asks after stopping the video.

"I don't know, chemotherapy? I'm sure there are pretty good antivirals for AIDS nowadays."

"You're wrong, Jack. The best treatment is always prevention. The best way to treat AIDS is to educate people about safe sex and the importance of getting tested. The best treatment for cancer is to teach people to avoid smoking and other carcinogens. If you could get everyone to live a healthy lifestyle you wouldn't get rid of cancer but you would eliminate much more of it than any medication ever did. Does this make sense?"

"Yeah, I understand. But what does this have to do with those kids?"

"All of the children that I just showed you are children with various degrees of neurological damage from their mothers being on drugs or drinking while pregnant. Do you think any of the things that they are doing at the hospital are going to help those kids?"

"I would imagine not much."

"You're right, Jack. They can try to make them more comfortable but a lot of those children are going to live lives of suffering. They are going to get worse and worse until one day they will die. So what do you think is the best treatment for these things, Jack?"

"Prevention, I guess."

"You're right. Prevention. The best way to reduce this kind of senseless suffering is to make sure that these people don't procreate to begin with."

"Okay. I see you your point. But—"

"Think about all of the murders out there, Jack. All of the innocent people out there who are killed every day for the contents of their wallets, or their cars. What do you think is the best treatment for this?"

"Prevention?"

"Yes! You're catching on. The people who grow up to commit these crimes don't usually come from loving families. They usually come from parents like our clients, Jack. Unfit parents. Or, they are raised in foster care which, I'm sorry to say, is a joke."

"So, you're saying that by finding the people who are most likely to have criminal children, or neurologically damaged children, and taking away their ability to reproduce, you are actually ridding the world of a lot of suffering."

"Exactly, Jack. Things have gotten out of hand in this world. Too many children are born to parents who are not capable of raising them. It's not these children's fault, Jack. We are not blaming the criminals. We have created them! We are simply trying to stop this endless cycle of madness. The twelve-step meetings, for instance. They seem like a good idea, right? Like maybe they help people deal with their addiction issues and live better lives? But think of it this way, Jack. If addiction is known to be genetic, why would you create an environment that brings them together? Go to any twelve-step meeting in the country and ask anyone where they met their husband or wife. An overwhelming majority of them will say AA or NA. What you are doing, essentially, is creating a breeding ground for the next generation of addicts. If anything, they should be kept far away from each other so that the genes and behaviors can be diluted out. What is the best treatment for addiction? You guessed it. Have I lost you, Jack?"

"No. Not at all. I'm just taking it all in. It's a lot to think about. So, what exactly do you do?"

"Well, we find people who have proven that they are not suitable parents and we make them an offer. We give them money, or help them out with their legal issues, in exchange for their ability to procreate. We don't force anything on them. The choice is ultimately theirs."

"Oh, okay. So my job would be prepping them for the operations and monitoring them in the recovery room then, right?"

"You got it."

"That is a lot to think about."

"It is. I know how it feels to be in your spot, believe me. That is why that is all I'm requiring of you today. You can go home. Have yourself a good weekend."

"Really? That's it?"

"That's it. Day one we usually like to explain everything then give our new hires some time to digest all of it. While our methods may seem cruel or even thuggish at times, you will come to learn that there is a reason for all of the things that we do. We are not cruel people, Jack. Our intentions are not bad. Our primary goal is to reduce suffering in the world and we keep that in mind when dealing with our employees as well."

"Okay, then. Thanks a lot. I appreciate everything. I guess I'll see you on Monday."

"Monday morning it is. You'll get your first patient. Have a good weekend, Jack."

"You too, Mr. Braxton."

I get out to my car and drive home. When I arrive I have no memory of having driven. My head is spinning and I need to lie down. I go inside my apartment and take Godzilla out for a walk in the heat. I'm sweating but I don't care.

I feel my phone vibrate in my pocket.

I take it out and look at the screen.

It's a missed call from Zeus.

CHAPTER TWELVE

Zeus tells me that he's picking me up later to go to a party. He doesn't seem concerned about whether or not I have plans or even any interest in going. When he tells me about the party I imagine the worst. I picture a house in the ghetto full of questionable characters, most of who are looking for trouble of some sort. I picture mounds of cocaine on tables and thick weed smoke in the air and heavy bass rattling the walls. I ask Zeus if I can bring my friend Bobby and he says it's okay. I'm going to need someone to talk to.

I call Bobby and he agrees to come before I finish asking.

I take a shower and put on the cleanest clothes that I've got and sit down to shoot up.

Just as the tiny needle penetrates my hungry vein and that beautiful bright red ribbon of blood shoots back into the syringe, I hear Bobby's moped pull right up to my door.

"Hang on a sec," I say, as Bobby knocks a hip-hop beat on my door.

I look back down at the syringe and watch the red blood cells dissipate and turn the clear solution pink. I push the plunger slowly and lean back in my chair. Bobby is still hammering the beat onto my door and I find myself nodding my head to the rhythm, forgetting for a moment that he is standing outside waiting for me to let him in.

"What are you doing in there, man? Jerkin off? Wrap it up, come on, let me in."

I open the door and Bobby walks in with a big smile. Godzilla jumps up into his arms and starts licking his face. I think that if Bobby were a dog, he would definitely be a Pug like Godzilla.

"So, where are we going tonight?"

"This dude, um, his name is Zeus, he—"

"Zeus? You know a guy names Zeus? Niiiiiiice."

"Yeah, well, he's gonna take us to a party. Not really sure what to expect."

"Who is this guy?"

"He's a coke dealer. I met him through a friend at the hospital."

"Aww yeah! So we're going to a coke party? We're gettin' crazy tonight, man!"

"Yeah, I'm assuming it's gonna be some kind of coke party. Might be in the ghetto, though. This guy is pretty hardcore. Be cool around him, okay?"

"Nothin' wrong with the ghetto, Jack. They know how to party over there. Say, can I get one of your Roxies?"

"Sure, help yourself. Only one or two, though, I'm running low."

Bobby gets to work crushing up a pill on my desk and I get out my laptop to check on Michelle. There really isn't any back and forth in my mind anymore about it. I know that I'm going to do it, and do it every day, and I've accepted this, as bad as it makes me feel afterwards.

I go straight to her page without looking at any other posts. There it is. It's official. Engaged. I stare at the word as the chemicals soar through my blood. The word hurts my eyes but the opiates turn the pain into a gentle, warm, tingling sensation. The ring sparkles in the picture and my vacant eyes absorb the light apathetically. This doesn't feel real.

I close my laptop after hearing the bass from Zeus' car in the parking lot. I remind Bobby again to be cool and I take a couple pills for the road.

We walk out of the apartment and Zeus is leaning against his car and talking on his phone while the music bumps inside. Turning down his music doesn't seem to be an option for Zeus. He sees us walking toward him and tells us to get in the car and that he needs to finish his phone call before we leave.

Bobby sits in the back with a big, goofy grin on his face. I know exactly what he's thinking. The tattoos. The teeth. I lean back between the seats and tell him not to mention anything about the tattoos. He gives me a sarcastic nod. Zeus opens the driver door and sits down in his seat. I introduce Bobby over the sound of the music.

"Zeus, this is Bobby, he lives down the street from me."

"Bobby, what's up, bruh? You ready to party?"

"What's up with those tattoos, man? How old were you when you got those?"

Fucking Bobby. He can't help himself.

"Sometime in my teens. Not sure exactly how old I was, bruh. Probably, sixteen, seventeen maybe."

"Why, though?"

"You ask a lot of questions don't you, homie? Tattoos are part of my culture, my lifestyle. Where I come from that's how you show what choo all bout, what choo stand for, ya heard."

"Yeah, okay. That's crazy, though."

"So," I interrupt the conversation. "Where are we going?"

"I gotta sell some shit at this party and we gonna chill there for a while. This fool is a doctor, bruh, his house is crazy. You gonna see some shit tonight."

A doctor? I wasn't expecting that.

We all get tired of trying to yell over the radio and just sit back and enjoy the drive.

Instead of driving into the ghetto, where I assumed we would go, we're driving toward one of the richest neighborhoods in Tampa.

The neighborhood is dark and quiet. The houses look like sleeping giants spread out on flawlessly manicured lawns. We pull into a large, circular driveway and park among ten or so other cars. All BMW's and Audis.

We step out of the car and Zeus goes back to his trunk and shamelessly takes out a Ziploc bag of white powder without trying to conceal it. He hands it to me and tells me to put it in my pocket with a big smile on his face. His silver teeth reflect the soft light from the front porch. I put the bag in my pocket and we walk up to the door. Zeus rings the bell. Thirty seconds later, the big, wooden door swings open and a skinny blonde woman with a huge, fake rack is standing in front of us. She's wearing a towel around her waist and a bikini top. I've never been too big on fake boobs but these are exceptional. Perfectly round and symmetrical.

Hypnotic. Her husband must be a plastic surgeon and, from the look of things, a good one.

"Come on in, Zeus baby, Abdul is in his play room waiting for you. Who are these handsome boys?"

"This here is Jack Lawrence, close personal friend of mine, and this here is his boi Bobby. They gonna chill with me a bit if that's alright with you."

"Sure, come on in."

The blonde woman steps aside and all three of us walk across the tile floor and into the living room. Dub-step music is coming from speakers mounted in the walls and ceiling creating an interesting contrast with the high-end décor. The furniture is all leather and the tables are solid oak. Everything looks heavy and expensive. I don't see a spec of dust.

"Where everybody at?" asks Zeus.

"Go on back to the pool room, hon. Everyone is back there."

Zeus opens a door near the kitchen and we walk down a dark staircase. The air is thick with smoke that smells like burnt plastic and cigars.

"Welcome!" says Abdul, the doctor, with his arms raised in the air. "Welcome, my friend, so glad you could join us."

Abdul is short and chubby. He is wearing a hideous, black toupee. His brown face is flushed with alcohol and whatever drug they're free-basing behind the bar in the corner of the room. There are no windows and the lighting is dim. The walls are all dark wood. I believe this is a proper "billiards room". The bar is fully stocked and the dub-step music is also playing down here. The men who are standing around the bar with Abdul all look like middle-aged doctors as well.

Zeus walks up to the group of men and starts shaking hands. They snicker behind his back when he's not looking and Abdul nods his head as if to say, "see I told you". Bobby and I join them and we are all introduced.

"What are you waitin' for, Jack? Show the man what we brought."

I look up and all of the men are looking at me. Oh yeah, the coke. I pull the bag out of my pocket and toss it onto the bar. All of the men's faces light up. Abdul pulls a wad of money out of his pocket and hands it to Zeus. Zeus counts it out on the bar with a serious look on his face.

"Perfect timing," says Abdul, as he walks over to the stairs. Four women are walking down wearing mini skirts, tube tops, and high heels. Definitely prostitutes.

Abdul walks the women over to the bar and one of the doctors starts dividing up lines of coke with a credit card on a large serving platter.

"I hope you guys are ready to have some fun tonight," says Abdul, while he grabs one of the girls' asses and looks the others up and down. The girl who got her ass grabbed pretends that she liked it and the other girls put on fake looks of jealousy, like they all want their asses grabbed as well.

We all finish our lines of coke and some of the men and women start disappearing into a dark theater room attached to the billiards room. I look over at Bobby who is beside himself with excitement and cocaine-fueled enthusiasm.

"Do you think we're going to get to fuck one of those prostitutes, man?" he asks me.

"I'm pretty sure we can if we want. You wanna go in that room and see what's up?"

"I'm game if you are."

Zeus is drinking a glass of liquor at the bar and talking once again on his phone. I meet his eyes and let him know that we are going into the room with the ladies. He smiles and nods his head.

Bobby and I walk into the dark room and there are big leather couches all facing a large screen that is currently displaying hardcore pornography.

A naked woman approaches us. Her torso is long and slender. Her tits are small and perky. Her thighs are pale and thick. She walks up to me and kisses me passionately on the lips and it feels good. It feels wonderful, actually. It's probably the coke talking but for a second I feel like I'm in love. Then I remember that these women are experts and that they kiss men like this by trade. Though I know in the back of my mind that the feelings aren't real, I let myself fall victim to her seduction. I grab the back of her head and kiss her back and then reach down and grab her ass. She lifts her leg up and wraps it around my back. Then, she stops kissing me and grabs Bobby by his shirt and pulls him in for a kiss. I rub her chest and belly and kiss her shoulders as Bobby kisses her lips. Then, she goes down to her knees and starts unzipping Bobby's pants and I look up at him. His goofy smile is contagious. I whisper to him that under no circumstances are we to make eye contact, nor are we to touch each other. He just smiles again and his eyes widen as the woman takes him into her mouth. He sits down on a couch while her head bobs up and down and I take her from behind. Just before I climax I think about the clinic for some reason. Then I hear a loud crash.

Bobby and I pull up our pants and rush into the billiards room.

Zeus has one of the men pinned up against the wall by his throat. The man's feet are off the ground.

"What the fuck, Zeus? What are you doing?" asks Abdul, who didn't even bother to zip up his pants. His toupee looks like it's about to fall off.

"Your boi here has a big fuckin' mouth, bruh. He got a little too much blow in him and started talkin' shit about my tattoos and my line of work. Didn't you, bruh?"

Zeus looks the man dead in his eyes and the man is terrified. Zeus, as usual, looks calm and collected.

The man doesn't speak. Zeus puts him down and tells us that it's time to go. On our way out we overhear the man call Zeus a "white trash thug" under his breath and two of the others giggle. Zeus turns around and walks back toward them.

I look over at Bobby.

We're both scared for the guy.

Zeus calmly walks up to the man, grabs him by the back of the neck with his left hand, and slams his right elbow into the side of his face. I immediately think occipital fracture as I see blood pouring out of the man's eye socket as he screams on the floor like a child. Another man grabs Zeus' arm and Zeus turns and easily breaks his nose with one punch. He looks at the other men with a smile on his face. He genuinely wants more. The men back away slowly. The prostitutes are peeking through the doorway.

We walk out to Zeus's car and drive back through the quiet neighborhood with the loud music blasting. Zeus smiles and puffs on a blunt like nothing happened.

CHAPTER THIRTEEN

I wake up to a knock at my door. An image of Zeus's face pops into my head but then I realize that the knocking is far too gentle to be him. Thank God.

I sit up and look around the room. Another image pops into my head. An image of Bobby's face while he was getting head from the prostitute that I was fucking from behind.

I'll probably avoid him for the next couple days, until the awkwardness wears off.

There is a feeling in my stomach that only co-caine users would understand. It's like the worst anxiety you've ever felt mixed with suicidal depression with a little nausea thrown in. I didn't really do anything that bad, aside from having unprotected sex with a prostitute, but I still feel like the scum of the Earth.

Oh well, what can you do?

I walk toward my front door. Godzilla is going insane barking.

Holy shit! It's her! It's Carrie! I have to hide everything.

I open one of the drawers of my desk and start sliding everything into it then I empty my ashtrays and throw out all of my empty beer bottles and cans.

"Coming. Just a minute," I yell at the door.

Okay, I think that's everything.

I open the door. She's standing in front of me wearing a bright yellow bikini top and a pair of Capri pants. I imagine a yellow thong underneath the pants. She has her hands resting on her soft, curvy hips. Her fingernails are painted yellow to match her bikini. She's wearing oversized sunglasses that are too dark for me to see her eyes. I pretend that she can't see me as I stare directly at her big, natural rack.

"Carrie, what's going on? What brings you here? How did you know where I—"

"Come on, Jack. Get your swim shorts, we're going to the beach."

"The beach? But—"

"Come on. I need some sun and I need some company. Unless you're too busy."

"No, no, no. I'm not too busy. Just need to take Godzilla out and get my suit on, that's all. I wasn't expecting company."

"You look like you had a rough night there, Mr. Lawrence."

"Yeah, I was out pretty late." I say, as she walks into my apartment. My eyes scour the living room looking for any evidence of drug use that I might have left behind.

"Well, come on then, let's go walk this sweet little puppy here then we can go."

She picks up Godzilla and lets him lick her face as I put on my sandals and a tank top then we walk to the front of the building and stand in the grass.

"Aren't you going to pick that up?" asks Carrie, after Godzilla relieves himself.

"No, I think shit is good for grass. I'm pretty sure using plastic dog shit bags is worse for the world than a little dog shit."

"Next time I ruin a pair of good running shoes stepping in someone's dog shit I'll try to remember that."

"Great, every time you see a pile of shit you're going to think about me now. Wonderful."

"Shut up, Jack. Let's go."

We get into her white convertible and drive to Clearwater beach. There isn't a cloud in the sky. She plays indie rock music, which is a nice break from the skull-crushingly loud rap music I listened to all night driving around with Zeus.

After we cross the causeway I ask her to stop by a gas station so I can pick up a six-pack of beer. I only now realized that I forgot to bring any pills.

It's hard to describe the panic that a true drug addict feels when he knows that he is not going to have any access to drugs for a while. For a true opiate addict, the need for the drug becomes an appetite every bit as real and as hard-wired into your brain as the need for air, food, or water. You're body gets deceived into believing that it needs the drug and it develops ways of motivating you to get it. Mostly by causing the worst feelings of pain, discomfort, and mental anguish you can imagine.

I'm nowhere near this point now but I will be soon. The alcohol, and hopefully the good company, will distract me.

I put the six-pack of tallboys into a plastic bag then walk over to the outdoor cooler in front of the gas station. I open the door, reach in, rip a small hole in one of the bags of ice, and grab two handfuls to keep in the bag with the beer. Carrie watches me and smiles while shaking her head disapprovingly.

We get to the beach, after driving around for a half hour looking for parking, and lay our towels out in the sand. I crack open one of my cold beers and take a long drink. She takes off her pants and I finally see the bottom half of her yellow bikini. It's not a thong but it's not much more than a thong. I choke on my beer a little when she bends down to get suntan lotion out of her bag. I bite my lip and think about smacking her fat, dimpled ass but I don't. I chug the rest of my beer and open another one.

Carrie lies down on her stomach and rests her chin on the back of her hands. I lie down beside her in the same position.

"So, you really want to know how I ended up working at New Beginnings?"

"Yeah, I mean, I wasn't going to ask again but, yeah."

"Come on."

"Where?"

"The water. We're going in."

I jog behind her as she skips over the hot sand toward the water. I watch all of the lotioned curves of her body bounce in the sunlight. I realize that I'm pretty much fully erect so I pick up the pace and dive in ahead of her.

We swim out past the breakers and make our way to the sandbar, which is fifty yards out.

"My mom had cancer. Bone cancer," she says, as we stand in water up to our shoulders.

"I'm sorry to hear that."

"She didn't have any insurance. She barely spoke any English, the poor lady. Her and my real father were both from Spain. My last name, Buck, I got from my step-dad who died in a car accident when I was twelve. My real father died when I was a baby. He was a drug addict. Anyways, like I said, she didn't have any insurance so she couldn't afford any of the drugs she needed. It's not like she was going to get any better, we all knew that she didn't have much longer. By that time the cancer had spread and there was really no hope for her, she just needed some of the drugs to make her feel better so that her last days weren't spent in agony. She was able to get pain meds pretty cheap from a doctor in town but what she really needed was Epogen. You know what that is, right?"

"Sure, yeah, the stuff that stimulates red blood cell production."

"Right, right. Well, I'm sure you know how expensive that stuff is then."

"Yeah, I've heard."

"It's insanely expensive. There was no way she was ever going to get any if I didn't do something. So, I took a vile. I was working oncology so I was handling it all the time. I just took a vile home and injected it into my mom and, I swear, it was like she came back from the dead. My brothers and I cried our eyes out when we saw the life back in her again. It was great. Needless to say, the next day I got more, then more the day after that. I couldn't stop. I didn't want to stop. Even now I don't regret what I did. By the time she died, I had stolen well over a hundred thousand dollars worth of Epogen. After she died that crazy motherfucker Zeus approached me and I was told about the clinic. The next day I told my boyfriend all about it even though they told me not to. The day after I told him, he disappeared. I never saw him again."

"Wow. You're a hero, Carrie. Jesus, here I am stuck in this shitty situation because I'm a selfish drug addict and you're here for doing something so selfless and admirable. I feel like a real scumbag right now."

"Let's get out, Jack."

We get out of the water and she tells me that she wants to stop by a used bookstore that is walking distance from the beach. Aside from drugs, books are my favorite things. Well, I guess I should probably say that they *were* my favorite things, since I don't do much reading anymore. The deeper I've gotten into the opiates the less I've cared about pretty much any of the things that used to make me happy. I'm thrilled that she is so excited about going to a bookstore but the beer and the distractions don't seem to be working. I can feel the weakness in my muscles and the buzzing in my nerves.

"Hey, do you mind if we just head back now? I'm feeling a little tired from all the sun and the beer."

"It's only a block away, Jack. We can go right after, I just need to pick up a new book."

I can't let her know how desperate I am.

"Okay. Sounds good."

Fuck.

We walk to the bookstore. It's a tiny little building across the street from the beach with a subtle, black and white sign that says Beach Reads. A few years ago this would have been heaven for me. I used to spend hours in places like this searching for those beautiful, yellow-paged, dog-eared, weak-spined, stale-cigarette-smelling gems that you can only find in a place like this. But right now all I can think about is shooting up. I know, how unfortunate.

We walk inside and Carrie waves at the guy behind the front counter and starts walking down the fiction isle.

I notice something familiar about the guy behind the counter. I can't quite put my finger on it. He's tall and tanned and in good shape. He has a short, neon-grey beard that glows against his dark skin. Little, metal glasses sit at the end of his nose. He's sitting on a stool looking down at an old book that has lost its cover.

"Can I help you with something?" he asks, after catching me staring at him.

"No. No thanks. Do I know you from somewhere?"

"I don't think so, buddy. Hey, are you okay? You look a little pale, like you're about to pass out."

"Yeah, I'm fine. Must have gotten a stomach bug or something."

"Stomach bug, huh?" he says incredulously.

"Yeah, must have eaten something bad."

He walks around the counter and looks me up and down.

"You know what I think, my friend?"

"What's that?"

"I think that you need something. I think that you need something that you should have never gotten yourself involved with in the first place. Do you know how I know that?"

"How?"

"I used to need the same things."

"Okay, I should probably be going. I'm going to go get my friend over there now."

"Hey," he says with his hand on my shoulder. "Take this business card. It has the number of the shop here on it. If you ever decide that you want to try to change things, call me."

"You want to take me to some twelve-step meeting or something? Be my 'sponsor'. No thanks, man. I appreciate your concern."

"No. Nothing like that. I think you're a lot like me. Those things aren't for people like us. Hell, they're no good for most people. My approach is a little different. You might find it helpful."

I take the business card and put it in my pocket and sarcastically thank him again for his concern. I have to admit that there is something intriguing about the man. He looks healthy, and, well, happy. Not happy like, joyously bouncing off the walls, more like, he has found something that works for him. Like he has found his place in the world. There is definitely something that this man has that I wouldn't mind having myself and I can't say that about many people.

Carrie pays for her paperback novel with cash and the man writes down the sale in a composition notebook. I just realized that there are no computers or even a cash register on the counter.

By the time we reach my apartment my muscles are starting to spasm and I am having a difficult time hiding it. Carrie can see how uncomfortable I am and has a look of concern on her face, which makes me sad. It's depressing when you see people feeling sympathy for you when you know that you are suffering from something that you did to yourself. You feel like you're deceiving them into feeling bad for you.

I assure her that it's just the sun and the beer that has me feeling sick even though I know that she can see through my bullshit. She drops me off and I hurry inside.

I snort a whole pill, swallow one, and then shoot one up while waiting for them to kick in. I light a cigarette and pass out with it still lit.

CHAPTER FOURTEEN

I wake up once again to a knock on my door. I'm seri-
ously considering moving off this goddamn island.
Apparently I'm very easy to find.

I look down at my lap and see my phone. The right
half of it is melted from falling asleep with a lit cigarette. This isn't the first time this has happened. I push
the button to illuminate the screen and realize that it's
eleven o'clock at night.

Shit, I must have only been out for a few hours.

Who the hell is knocking at my door at eleven
o'clock?

I try to stand up with Godzilla's dead weight on my
legs. He's lying on his back with his fat belly in the air,

snoring. I pick him up gently and put him back down on the couch and walk toward the door. It doesn't look like anyone is there. Maybe, hopefully, it was a dream.

I unlock the door and open it slowly. The humid air rushes through the crack in the door and paints my face with a layer of moisture. I look around. I see bugs circling an outdoor light. Otherwise, I see no movement. No life. Must have been a dream.

I look down at the ground before closing the door and see a piece of paper with big, red letters that say, "Read me". I unfold the paper and there is one sentence written in black pen. It says, "Go to the dog beach right now, alone". That's all it says.

The dog beach? Why would someone want me to go to the dog beach at eleven at night?

Considering the events of the past couple days I decide that I should probably follow the instructions on the note. I mean, I am involved with people who apparently kill people who don't do as their told.

I put on my clothes, kiss Godzilla, swallow two pills, and then drive down Davis Boulevard to the dog beach at the end of the island.

There are no cars parked in the parking lot. I sit in my car and smoke a cigarette, waiting for someone to show up. No one comes. I get out and walk through the gate and step onto the beach.

A hundred yards up the beach is a picnic table where Tom, Bobby, and I used to set up shop when we would spend the evening out here drinking. I'm looking toward the picnic table and it looks like someone is sitting on top of it but I can't be certain.

"Hey! Hey, you! Are you waiting for me?"

No answer. However, I did see the figure move and am now certain that there is someone sitting there. I walk closer and can see that the person on the table is wearing all black. Black pants and a black, hooded sweatshirt with the hood pulled over his or her head. All I can think about is how hot this person must be.

I walk closer and notice that there is a Jet Ski floating in the black water.

"Hey. Are you the one who left that creepy note at my door?"

No response. I'm starting to get annoyed.

"Hey, I'm talking to you. Are you the one who left—?"

What the fuck? The person turns around and beneath the hood I see a mask. It looks like a black, rubber cat's face with long, nylon whiskers.

I jump back and stumble over a rock.

The person stands up and walks over to the Jet Ski, sits on it, and starts it up.

"You want me to follow you?"

The engine revs up and I assume this means yes.

I climb onto the back and keep my hands by my side. I think about Carrie and her black motorcycle and how I had never been on a motorcycle or a Jet Ski until a couple days ago.

"Take your phone out of your pocket."

It's a man's voice. He's trying to disguise it, but it still sounds familiar.

"You want me to give you my—"

"Take your phone out of your pocket and go put it on the picnic table. You can't take it with you."

I climb off the Jet Ski and walk back to the table. Instead of putting it on the table I hide it in a pile of rocks nearby then I get back on the Jet Ski.

The engine whines and a stream of water shoots up into the air behind us as we fly out into the bay, skipping across the black, vinyl surface of the water.

Just as I start to lose myself in the thrill of the speed and the beauty of the water at night I notice a large drainage tunnel ahead that we seem to be driving toward with no sign of slowing down. In fact, the Jet Ski is driving faster as we get closer to the tunnel, which is half in the water and half out. The driver turns on a makeshift headlight that is strapped to the front of the Jet Ski and tells me to watch my head. We're going in and at this point there isn't much I can do about it aside from jumping off, which would leave me swimming alone in the bay in the middle of the night. This is going to happen. It's happening.

Oh my God!

I close my eyes and duck my head as we speed into the tunnel. The sound of the engine is multiplied by a thousand with the metal all around us. I peek over the man's shoulder and watch the headlight illuminate the dark, wet tunnel that we are barreling down at near full speed. I close my eyes again. It's too much. It's too fast. It's too loud. I should be in bed right now.

We stop and I open my eyes.

I'm in a clearing. A large, smelly, concrete room somewhere underneath downtown Tampa. There are several lights lighting up an area with a desk made out of PVC buckets and wood scraps. There are two laptops on the desk that are on. Where is the electricity coming from? Where am I? Another person wearing a black cat mask approaches and helps us off the Jet Ski. Two more people emerge from the shadows, all wearing masks.

"Okay, what is this? Who are you people?"

One of the cat-faced people approaches me and tells me to sit down on an old lawn chair near the desk. Whoever these people are, they seem to be pretty resourceful. I look around and I feel like I'm in a clubhouse pieced together with whatever junk they found floating around the bay.

"We are a group of people who know the truth about New Beginnings and the Bright Futures division.

Most of us are victims of those tyrants that you now work for."

"Hey, listen, I just started, I just found out what they do, I have nothing to do with any of this."

"Calm down, Jack. We're not blaming you for anything. We're not here to hurt you. Most of us are people who have gone against the clinic and have had everything taken from us. They killed our families, our friends. We have nothing to lose."

"I'm really sorry to hear that, but why are you telling me this?"

"We are going to take them down, Jack. The whole thing. We are going to take it down and expose them. All of them. And—"

"And what?"

"And, we need your help. We need people on the inside."

"You think that I'm going to help you? Come on, man, do you have any idea who these people are? What they're capable of? I mean, you're all lucky to be alive right now."

"This isn't much of a life, Jack. We all live our lives in hiding, in seclusion, never knowing how or when they are going to find us and do to us what they have done to our families."

"I think you have the wrong person. I would like to help you guys, and I'm sorry for what you've been through, I really am, but I just can't handle any more stress in my life right now. Don't worry, your secret is safe with me, I promise I won't tell anyone about any of this."

"Look, Jack, we have taken a very big risk by bringing you here. We were told by several reliable sources that you are one of the good ones. At this point you are either with us or against us. We cannot afford to have anyone out there who knows about us who isn't with us. Do you understand?"

"What, so, you're telling me that since I know about you guys I have no choice but to work with you? I've been hearing this a lot lately and I'm really sick of it. I'm tired of people telling me that I have to do this, or that, it's fucking crazy! I didn't ask for any of this!"

"Don't play innocent, Jack. We know about you. You are far from innocent."

"Whatever. Okay, so, I guess I don't have a choice then do I? What is it you want me to do?"

One of the cat-faces kneels down beside me and places their hand on my knee as I sit with my face in my hands.

"Jack."

It's a female voice. I look up.

"Jack, look at me."

I see the mask peel away revealing a face behind it. A beautiful face. It's Carrie.

I pass out.

CHAPTER FIFTEEN

It must have been a mixture of the drugs and the stress and the Jet Ski ride. I've nodded out plenty of times but never just passed out cold like that. All I remember is seeing Carrie's face then being dragged back onto the Jet Ski. When I opened my eyes one of the masked men told me that they would be in touch and that now was probably not the best time to talk. I'm actually glad that I passed out to tell you the truth. I'm not sure if I can handle any more right now.

I get to the apartment and plop down on my couch. Godzilla climbs onto my chest and licks the salt off of my face and I'm too exhausted to care.

What have I gotten myself into?

Things used to be so simple when Michelle and I were together. Grocery shopping, decorating the apartment, taking Godzilla to the park, these are the things that I find myself thinking about. The simple things. The way that she would hold onto my arm while we walked down the isles at the grocery store because her hands would get cold. I miss that. I even miss our stupid arguments. How dramatic we would get over silly little things and then laugh about it later.

What do I have now?

Drugs? Alcohol? A shitty apartment that smells like piss and a weird-smelling sweat from all the chemicals I put into my body?

The only thing that I truly care about right now is Godzilla, and, to tell you the truth, I think that he would be better off without me.

Come to think of it, I'm sure a lot of people would be better off without me.

I wonder if I have it in me to end it all. I've thought about it a few times but never truly considered it.

Just the thought of fading out and being done with all of this just caused a wave of relief to come over me.

I don't know why I never considered it before. It makes so much sense. If anyone out there has a good reason to commit suicide it's me. I'm pretty sure that if people found out what I was going through they would understand.

I'm going to do it. And you know what? I'm not even sad about it. I feel good about this decision. I feel like I'm finally doing something constructive with my life. A selfless act. If there is a God up there, I'm sure he or she is behind me in this.

First, I send a text to Myka telling her that I might not be able to care for Godzilla for much longer and then ask her if she can stop by in the morning to pick him up. Then, I turn off my phone so I don't have to explain. I figure this will jar her curiosity enough to get her to stop by in the morning. I do feel bad about causing her to be the one to find my body but she *is* a nurse. A good, tough nurse. I know she can handle it without too much psychological damage.

I go into my medicine cabinet and scrounge up as many benzodiazepines as I can find. All I have are two Klonopins and one Xanax. This should be enough, though. Just about every overdose on opiates I've seen in the hospital is from someone mixing them with benzos. I'm sure what I have is more than enough to get the job done.

I sit down at my desk and swallow the benzos. I open my bottle of pills and realize that there are only five left. I can't believe I've taken almost all of them already. I must have given some away or lost some. No way I took that many pills. I swallow four of them with a large shot of chilled vodka from my freezer and then chase that with a beer. I crush up the last pill and dump the powder into the charred bottle cap that I use to cook up. I add a syringe full of tap water. I hold it up with the pliers and bring the water to a boil. I drop in the cigarette filter and watch it expand. I draw up the solution into the syringe. I swallow the filter like a pill with another shot of vodka. I turn around in my chair and see Godzilla sleeping on the couch. His tongue is sticking out of his mouth and he is snoring. I think back to the day that Michelle and I brought him home and how it took months for me to get used to that sound. Now I have a hard time sleeping when I *don't* hear his little snorts. Funny how things change.

I walk over to Godzilla and give him a big kiss on his wet nose and squeeze his fat face in my hands. He opens his eyes for a second then closes them.

I walk back over to my desk, sit down, and tie my arm off with the ACE bandage.

The vein expands and begs me for the needle.

I slide it in slowly, savoring the sting.

A thick, red jellyfish appears in the clear solution and I watch it float around and dissolve.

I push the plunger slowly and my senses start to fade. My vision narrows.

I stumble to the bed that I haven't slept in since Michelle left and fall face down on the mattress.

Myka. I should have known that she would intervene. According to the nurse that I see when I wake up, Myka came to my apartment after receiving my text. She saved my life.

I look around the room and realize that I'm in the same hospital where I used to work. Luckily, I don't know the nurse who is currently in my room taking my vital signs and she doesn't seem to know me.

I have to get out of here.

The nurse finishes my vitals and asks if I need anything. I say no. She walks out of the room.

I pull out my IV line and sit up in bed.

I hold a washcloth up to the puncture wound until it stops bleeding.

I pull back the divider curtain and see that I don't have a roommate.

The door to my room opens and Mr. Braxton walks in.

"Mr. Braxton? What are you—?"

"Sit down."

I sit down.

"Suicide is not an option for you, Mr. Lawrence. Perhaps I should have made that clear from the beginning. If you choose to kill yourself, we will send Zeus to see your friends, your ex-girlfriend, your family, and even your dog. Are we clear now, Jack?"

"You're sick. You're all fucking insane, sick people."

"Calm down, Jack. I know that it's hard to accept the position that you are currently finding yourself in. Hell, it would be hard for anyone to deal with. But you *will* deal with it and you *will* accept it. You do not have any other option. You have gotten yourself into this. I am checking you out of here right now and driving you home. I can't have you hanging out around here."

"Can you even—?"

"I can do whatever I want, Jack. Put your clothes on and follow me."

I put on my clothes and walk out with Mr. Braxton.

I stand behind him like a timid child as he signs discharge papers. No one seems concerned that he's not related to me. I try my best to hide my face but I do make eye contact with one nurse and one PCT who I know recognize me. They don't say anything and neither do I. I'm sure everyone on the floor will be happy to have something to gossip about for the rest of the week. Glad I could help.

Mr. Braxton drives me home and tells me that he expects me to be at work as scheduled.

The first thing I do when I get inside is call Myka. She doesn't answer. She's probably pissed off at me, and rightly so. I would be pissed off too if someone decided to force me into taking part in their suicide attempt. I'll give her a day or two to cool off.

I give Godzilla a big kiss and take him out for a walk.

I reach into my pocket to find a lighter and feel the business card I got from the guy at the used bookstore. I look at his name and realize that I am all out of pills.

I dial his number.

He picks up.

I ask him if he remember me.

He says that he does.

I tell him that I think that I need help.

He asks me if I *want* help.

I tell him that I do.

He tells me to meet him at the bookstore.

I tell him that I'll come by after my first day of work.

PART 4

CHAPTER SIXTEEN

Ok, first real day at the new job. How the hell am I going to do this? I have no pills left and I don't have time to go to the pill-mill. Come to think of it, I probably don't have insurance anymore and I definitely don't have enough money to buy the pills without it. This just keeps getting worse by the moment. I've heard that this is how a lot of people end up on heroin. The pills become too expensive and you realize that you can get the same, or a better, high for half the price. It does make sense. It's weird how stigmas fade away as you continuously lower your standard of living. Heroin used to be such a heavy and ugly word with grotesque images attached to it. Now it almost seems stupid if I *don't* use heroin. I've come a long way.

I know for a fact that I will not be able to function unless I take something. It's not that I need to get high, it's just that I need to not feel like ripping the skin off my face.

I call Zeus and he agrees to meet me in the parking lot before I go into work.

I take a shower and I'm almost too weak to hold the soap.

I take Godzilla out for a walk and my fingers are almost too weak to light my cigarette.

The sun hurts my skin. I can smell the chemicals leaking out of my pores and I can taste them in my mouth. My stomach knots up every time a person passes by and I think about engaging in any form of social interaction. I've gotten to the point that, without the drugs, I am no longer human. I can no longer function as a human being. Without the drugs I am some kind of nocturnal, parasitic creature that smells terrible and lacks the ability to communicate or interact.

My posture is terrible.

My hair is a mess.

I go back inside and put on my scrubs with the long sleeve undershirt to hide my track marks then I leave for work.

Zeus is waiting for me in the parking lot. He is sitting inside his car smoking and rapping as usual. He sees me and he shows me his big silver teeth as he nods his head and waves his hands back and forth like he's rapping the lyrics directly to me.

I walk up to his window and he looks at me for a second before speaking.

"Why you let yourself get like this, bruh?"

"Like what?"

"Like *this,* homie," he says, as he points at me with a disappointed look on his face.

"I don't know what you're talking about. I just need some pills before I go to work."

"You a fuckin' junkie, bruh. You need to respect yourself. You look like a bitch right now."

"Look, man, I just texted you to see if you had any pills. I don't want to get into this right now. If you don't have anything than fuck off. I don't need this shit from some wanna-be thug, or whatever you are."

What have I done? The withdrawals have me so miserable that I forgot who I'm talking to.

Zeus gets out of the car, sets his blunt down on the ground, then punches me in the stomach.

I drop to the hot asphalt, gasping for air. Fuck, I can't breath! I think my fucking lung is collapsed! Shit.

The pain passes as my diaphragm relaxes and allows me to breathe.

Zeus is standing over me. He bends down and picks up his blunt then opens his car door. He reaches into his console and pulls out a baggie filled with big, white pills and throws it on my chest.

"Next time I'm gonna knock your teeth out, bruh."

He gets back into his car and spins his tires as he speeds out of the parking lot in a cloud of burnt rubber smoke.

I hold the pills up to the sunlight. I'm still lying on my back. Percocet. It's not what I wanted, but if I take enough I should be able to keep the withdrawals from getting too bad.

I go back to my car and swallow five pills with a sip of hot beer then smoke a cigarette while I wait for them to kick in.

The woman at the front desk hands me a badge when I walk in. It has my name on it and she tells me that it will allow me access to all of the doors leading down to the Bright Futures area. There is a tiny set of keys attached to the badge that she tells me will unlock the elevator that leads to the basement. She looks me up and down after I take the badge and clip it to my scrubs, like she wants to ask me something, but she doesn't say anything.

I wave my badge over a box near the big, brown door and it swings open automatically. Just as I walk through the threshold the pills start to kick in and I find myself smiling. It is a feeling beyond relief. Like a big lung full of air to a drowning man. I think about the man that I am supposed to call and meet up with after work and I feel silly for even calling him in the first place. Why would I ever want to get rid of this? Why would I ever want to stop feeling like this? As the chemicals flood my brain I look around at all of the employees walking around, working, eating, going about their days completely sober, and I feel bad for them. What a horrible way to go through life. I'm going to stick with the drugs. Nothing feels as good as the way I feel right now.

"Jack."

I turn around and Carrie is standing behind me.

"Carrie. Hey, what's up? You look—"

"Come on, Jack."

She walks past me and I follow her to the elevator. She tells me to try out my elevator key and I do. I can't stop smiling and she knows that something is going on.

We get in the elevator and I start to speak and she gives me a look that silences me immediately. I realize that there will never be any cordiality between us during business hours.

Before we get off the elevator she stands close to me and tells me to call her after work and that she needs to talk to me.

She shushes me before I can respond.

We walk down the same boring hallway that leads to Mr. Braxton's office but this time we walk past his door to a steel double-door. Carrie points to a box on the wall and I wave my badge over it. The door opens and we are now in the Bright Futures division of New Beginnings.

A woman named Brenda is the charge nurse. She is a short, stocky woman, probably in her mid fifties. She walks me to one of the rooms and hands me a maroon chart. She tells me to read the patient's history before I introduce myself then she gives me a handful of individually packaged pills.

"These are the patient's morning meds, Nurse Jack. Do you think you can handle this?" she says sarcastically. There is a sincere warmth behind her sarcasm. She looks at me almost motherly.

"Yeah, I think I can handle it."

"Good. Give the morning meds and start an IV on her. She's going for a procedure later. Oh, and Jack, we keep very close tabs on all of the meds here and there are cameras everywhere. Just a heads up."

"What do you mean? I wouldn't, I mean, I—"

"Just watch yourself, Jack. That's all."

"Thanks, Brenda."

I put the pills in my pocket and look at the chart. White female, twenty-three years old, two children who the state has custody of, long history of drug abuse, multiple arrests. This should be fun.

I walk into the room and the woman is sitting up in bed watching television. She is filing her fingernails and talking to someone on speakerphone. She looks happy to be here. I was expecting an emotional train wreck. This woman looks like she's waiting in line at Disney World.

"Where my pills?" she asks without ending her call or even looking up. She has a trailer park twang and an undeserved look of entitlement on her face.

"Can you get off your phone? I need to do a quick assessment before giving you your pills."

"No, nah, you ain't gotta do no assessment, go on and get me the other nurse, you don't know what choo doin'."

"Listen. This is my first day here. Could you just work with me?"

She mistakes my malaise with genuine concern and agrees to hang up her phone.

I thank her then I get to work taking her vital signs.

"So, what brings you here?" I ask.

"My sister needs a surgery or the doctors say she gonna die. I'm doin' this so these people will pay for her surgery."

I look at her face as she tells me the sob story and I don't believe a word of it. The track marks on her arms tell me that she has every intention of using the money to buy drugs. I wonder how much she's getting?

The veins in her arms are too banged up for an IV so I put one in her left wrist, which she doesn't mind at all.

As I thread her vein with the needle I look up at her face and can't help but feel like we are doing the world a favor by not allowing this woman to reproduce any more. I hate to say it, because it sounds so cold and callused, but it's true. I think about my own arms and how they look almost identical to hers.

I think about the guy at the bookstore and I reconsider calling him.

The day went by smoothly. After the first few patients I got into the swing of things and it became a job like any other. Working in the hospital I came across things every day that I didn't agree with but that never stopped me from doing my job. Halfway through the day I was no longer taking part in an experiment in eugenics, I was merely prepping people for surgery and monitoring them afterwards.

Carrie approaches me as I walk out to my car after my shift is over. She tells me that she wants to talk to me and I tell her that I'm going to go to Beach Reads later and that maybe we can meet up there. She agrees and tells me to text her when I get there.

CHAPTER SEVENTEEN

I arrive at the bookstore and pop two pills before I walk in. There are no cars in the parking lot. I learned from our phone conversation after I got out of work that the man's name is Ben Ellsworth. He looks like a Ben.

I walk through the door and a bell that is attached to the door handle jingles. A black cat jumps off the front counter and runs full speed into a back room. I look around the shop and don't see anyone. I close my eyes and breathe in the moldy smell of old books. It relaxes me.

I hear a toilet flush in the back then I see Ben emerge from behind a curtain.

"Jack. So glad you came. You want a cup of coffee? I just made a pot."

"Sure, I'll have a cup."

"Come on in and sit down, man, there's a seat for you there behind the counter. I found this old chair at a garage sale the other day. Got it for ten bucks. I had to sand and re-finish the legs and re-upholster the cushions, but it was worth it."

I take the cup of coffee and sit down in the chair. The soft, green fabric tickles my legs. Ben sits up on his stool and blows on his coffee then takes a sip.

"So, you're thinking about getting your shit together, huh?"

"Yeah. Do you own this place? Is this all yours?"

"Yeah, I bought it, umm, I guess it was probably about fifteen years ago now."

"It's nice here. I would love to work at a place like this. Seems so peaceful."

"It's not bad. I live upstairs, too. This is my world, man."

"Nice."

"Are you married?"

"Pretty much. I've been with the same woman for twenty years."

"Any kids? Sorry about all the questions."

"It's okay, I don't mind. No, no kids of my own. My lady has a few that I pretty much raised, though. I call them my daughters. They're all out on their own now."

"Oh, okay."

I look around the room and sip my coffee. I'm a little embarrassed that I asked him so many questions for some reason. Maybe it's the combination of the pills and the coffee that has me talking a lot. Or maybe I'm just really interested in this guy's life.

"How are you feeling today? When I saw you the other day you didn't look so good."

"I'm okay now. A little better."

"Opiates. Am I right? You look like an opiate guy. Pills? Heroin?"

"Yeah, opiates. I'm a nurse so I got into intravenous pain meds when I was working at the hospital. I got fired recently so I've been pretty much sticking with pills. I do shoot them up sometimes, though."

"Wow. A male nurse. Good for you. Sorry to hear about your job."

"It's better this way. If I had stayed there I probably would have ended up hurting someone."

"You're probably right. These things tend to get worse before they get better."

"What drugs were you into? If you don't mind me asking."

"Pretty much everything, really. Heroin was the biggest but I like cocaine a lot, I drank a lot too, and pills were always part of the equation."

"How did you stop? Did you go to rehab?"

"I went to a few different rehabs. Court ordered. I went to twelve-step meetings, all of that. I wasn't really into it. The problem was that I didn't see anything in those people that I wanted for myself. It's hard to take advice from people if you don't want to be anything like them, you know? Even though what they're saying might sound good, in the back of your mind you're thinking that the best you are going to achieve by following them is to get where they are. And if you don't like where they are, or who they are, it's hard to really listen to them."

"I know exactly what you mean."

"For instance, I grew up in a small town where everyone was Christian. Everyone except for my parents. People would tell me all the time, not in these exact words, but they would tell me that if I wasn't like them, then I was going to burn in hell for eternity. The problem with that was that I had no interest in being anything like them. I'm not saying that they were bad people, I just didn't want to be like them, so it was hard for me to listen to what they were telling me because I had made up my mind that I would rather burn than be like them. The twelve-step meetings are exactly the same. The people are nice enough and they do have some good things to say, but ultimately, I don't want what they have. I never did. And just like the Christians, they see their leader as 'divinely appointed' so it's really a waste of time to try and convince them that you're not interested. Bill Wilson, the founder of AA, figured out how to

Male Nurse

use the same techniques as the Christians when he created his institution. First, tell people that they are fundamentally flawed. Beat them down basically. In Christianity they tell people that they are born sinners. In AA they tell people that they are diseased and that they are weak and helpless against the drugs or alcohol. Then, they offer themselves as your one and only path to redemption. It's kind of sadistic if you think about it. You find people who are suffering, who are looking for help, and you tell them that they are pathetic and worthless, basically reinforcing the way that they already feel about themselves, and then you tell them that you can save them. It reminds me of an abusive relationship where the man constantly reminds the woman that she is ugly and stupid and that no one will ever want her other than him. And the girl learns to believe the guy and cling to him no matter how destructive the relationship is. That's what I saw in Christianity and in the twelve-step programs. People being told that they are stupid and weak and worthless so that they become more and more dependent on the institution. Now, I do think that these institutions do help some people, probably a lot of people, but I'm just not one of them. I think that very extroverted people benefit the most from the twelve-step meetings. The people who like an audience, those are the people who get the most out of them. They tell you to speak up and talk about your problems to a group of strangers and act like there is something wrong with you when you tell them that you don't want to. There are people who feel better after discussing their problems with a group of strangers and there are people who don't. I don't."

"So, what did you do? How did you get clean?"

"I wrote a new story for myself. The people in the meetings, even the ones with forty years clean, are still living in the same story. The story where they are the drug addict or the alcoholic, only now they are an addict who is clean, or 'in recovery'. They relive those days over and over year after year because that is who they are. They're stuck, forever standing at a dead end road. I chose to write a new story. Create a new character. The Ben Ellsworth that was addicted to heroin is gone. I replaced him with a Ben Ellsworth who lives a healthy lifestyle, mentally and physically. I didn't surround myself with other addicts, I surrounded myself with people whose lives didn't revolve around substances at all. What I did was the opposite of what the meetings teach you. I empowered myself. They told me that I was weak and powerless, I told myself that I was strong and powerful. I built up my confidence by proving them wrong. Exercise became a big part of my life as I learned that that helped with my confidence. They told me that it wasn't my fault, that I was the victim of a disease, I chose to own up to my mistakes and not to see myself as the victim of anything. They told me to put myself first, like I hadn't been doing that my whole life, and I chose to put my family first and to think about others when making decisions and how they would affect them. I put an image in my mind of a Ben Ellsworth who was happy and healthy. I thought about what kind of life would make me truly happy and I took steps every single day towards creating that life for myself. Getting off drugs was the easy part. See, what the drugs do, and this goes for a lot of legal drugs as well, is, they help you tolerate a life that you might otherwise find repulsive. It's much easier to change the way you feel about your life with drugs than it is to change your life. I had to get to work building a whole new world to live in. A world that I didn't need or want to escape."

"And this is the life that you built?"

"Exactly. I always loved used books. I always loved the beach. I wake up every day now, go for a long run on the beach or a swim in the ocean or go on a bike ride, then I come home, shower, drink coffee and read, then open up shop. No drinking, no drugs, no drama. I have a beautiful wife and a few close friends that I go fishing with occasionally. I would say that I am happier than I ever thought that I could be."

"Do you think that I could do that?"

"I know you can do it. If I can, anyone can. You just have to change your attitude. You have to think of a new story to live. A story with a happy ending instead of the story you're in now, which is definitely a tragedy."

"I just don't think that I can quit the drugs. It's so painful."

"Toughen the fuck up. You can handle it. And don't bother with any of the rehabs either. They make things way too comfortable. You need to feel this. You need to feel the full extent of what you've done to yourself. You've crippled yourself mentally, physically, emotionally, spiritually, and probably financially. Think about all the people in this world who don't have the luxury of crippling themselves. The people who wake up every day with problems that aren't as easily solved as ours. We are lucky in that respect. There is no easy way out, my friend."

"Shit. I guess I could give it a shot."

"Do it. If you do, I promise one day you will look back and realize that it was the best decision of your life. But hey, the old ball and chain is about to be here and we're going out to dinner."

"Oh, yeah, okay. Yeah, I needed to head out anyways."

"But listen, you can stop by any time. You know where to find me. I'm always here."

"Yeah, okay. I might take you up on that."

"When you decide to stop the drugs and things start to get ugly give me a call. I'll try to talk you through it if I can."

"Okay. Thanks."

He pats me on the shoulder and walks to the back room. I walk out to my car and text Carrie.

Do I really think that I can do this? It just doesn't seem possible for some reason. Quitting drugs feels like quitting food or water. It's hard to picture myself living without them. I suppose I could get myself through this week at work then try to quit this weekend. My head hurts just thinking about it.

I walk across the street to the beach and sit in the sand while I wait for Carrie to show up.

CHAPTER EIGHTEEN

Carrie sneaks up behind me and grabs my shoulders. I flinch and my lit cigarette falls into my lap. I jump up and swat the embers off my shorts as she laughs. The sun is starting to set and my eyes were lost in the pink rays swaying over the calm water. Sunsets on the ocean really are amazing. There is a five-minute window just before the sun disappears that the world stops moving. I was there, in that moment, just before I was jolted out of it by this beautiful woman who is now standing beside me laughing.

"I am so sorry, Jack. I'll get you a new pair of shorts."

"No you won't. That was messed up. Didn't you see that I was in a moment there?"

"Yeah, I did. That's why I couldn't help myself."

She's wearing a coral-colored sundress that accents her curves and I can see the lines of her bikini underneath it. Her hair is tied up in a bun, showcasing her long, smooth neck.

"I'm assuming we're going in."

"If you want to talk, then, yeah. That's the only place I feel safe, Jack. Sorry."

"No, trust me, I don't mind. You think it bothers me to have an excuse to see you in a bikini whenever I want?"

"Shut up, Jack. What were you doing at the bookstore by the way?"

"Last time I was there with you, the owner guy gave me his business card and told me to give him a call."

"Ben? Why?"

"Let's just say that he recognized something in me that he struggled with at one point in his life. I don't want to talk too much about the man's business."

"Okay. Wow, Ben, I love that guy. I've been going there for years, he's such a cool man, and him and his wife are so cute. Did you meet her?"

"No. We just talked in the shop for a while before he closed up. He is pretty cool."

"Well, hopefully whatever you guys talked about was helpful. He seems to have his shit together, and you, my friend, do not."

"No I do not."

"Okay, lets hop in."

"You do know that this is prime feeding time for sharks, right?"

"Are you scared, Jack?"

"No, I'm just saying that…"

She takes off her sundress and my voice trails off. I silently thank God for the little bit of light that is left. This time it's a white bikini. It's even smaller than the yellow one. Dear God I don't know how much more of this I can take.

We wade out into the warm water then both dive in after we count down from three.

We emerge and stand face to face with the water coming up to our necks. She's so close that I can feel her breath. I slowly reach my hands out and she lets me hold onto her hips and pull her in closer to me. She wraps her legs around my back and we bounce up and down with the swells, looking each other in the eye. She smiles and wraps her arms around my neck and I lean in for a kiss. She hesitates for a moment then submits. The kiss is long and slow and passionate. I haven't had a kiss with this much feeling behind it in a very long time, aside from the prostitute, but that wasn't real. I find myself holding back tears for some reason after the kiss is over and we are once again standing face to face, tangled up in each other's wet limbs.

"We're animals, Jack. All of us. We were never meant to be perfect. We were simply meant to be human. I can see the good that the clinic does. I will admit that they do, do a lot of good. But where does it end? Don't you think that this is a dangerous path for us to be going down?"

"I don't know, Carrie. To be honest with you, I'm very confused about all of this. I don't know how I feel anymore. I can see things from both sides, really. It's just hard for me to focus on these big issues when my personal life is such a mess. I feel like, before I can make any clear decisions about how I feel, or even who I am, I need to straighten some things out. These people are forcing me to feel one way, now you guys are forcing me to feel another way, and the whole time all I can really think about is what a mess I've made of my life."

"I understand. And I'm sorry that I have brought you into this, I really am. But they need more people on the inside. Right now I'm the only one. I can't do it alone."

"Do what?"

"They'll explain soon. They have been working on a plan to make things right. They need our help."

"If it's for you, if I'm doing this to help *you*, that makes things easier for me. That is something I can wrap my mind around a little easier. If you need me to go along with whatever these people are up to, then I would be happy to help."

"Thank you, Jack."

She unwraps her legs, grabs my hand, and starts leading me out of the water. The evening breeze is cold on my skin but it feels nice. After we're out of the water and standing in the wet sand she pulls me in for another kiss. She bends her knees as we kiss and I follow her to the ground where we make love beneath the stars. I had forgotten how nice it is to "make love" to someone. To be aroused by the feelings and emotions between myself and another person. When I feel myself building up to a climax I whisper a subtle hint into her ear that I am about to cum. I start to pull out and she wraps her legs and arms tightly around me and holds me to her body, leaving me no choice but to cum deep inside of her.

After it's over, we lay on our backs looking up at the stars, naked.

CHAPTER NINETEEN

Carrie actually smiles when she sees me walk into work. Not a grin either or a smirk, it was a dead on smile, like she was happy to see me. As I look at her face I feel a strange sensation. It's a happiness that is trying to emerge from below the chemicals. Some cocktail of hormones being released into my system that actually feels better than the drugs.

I have enough Percocets in my system to ward off the withdrawals but not enough to be high. I did the math this morning and realized that I have just enough to last me until Friday if I keep up with the doses that I'm giving myself now. As miserable as I know that it's going to be, I'm kind of excited about this weekend.

I'm looking at it like I would imagine a marathon runner looks at a big race. He knows that the run is going to be miserable and treacherous but he also knows how wonderful the feeling of accomplishment will be at the end. That's what I'm focused on. An image in my mind of myself standing tall without any substances in my system. Like Ben said, I have to write a new character for myself. The character that I am writing is strong and confident. He takes care of his health and his woman. And by woman I mean Carrie.

This morning when I woke up I instinctually grabbed my laptop to check up on Michelle. I turned on the computer and went to Facebook but stopped myself before clicking on her page. That's a pretty big success for me. If I'm strong enough to avoid cyberstalking my ex, I think I might be able to handle the drugs.

I walk over to the nurse's station and grab my first patient's chart. The work here really is pretty easy. If you can dissociate yourself with the bigger picture of what you're doing and just focus on whatever task is at hand, it's not so bad. Kind of monotonous, actually.

The hardest part for me now is that I see too much of myself in my patients. When most people look at addicts they see someone who is selfish and lazy and inconsiderate. All of these judgments are one hundred percent accurate, but what most people don't take into consideration is the backstory. Becoming an addict doesn't just happen overnight. It happens after a long series of exponentially poor decisions that usually stem from some traumatic event. Kind of like how I was convinced the other day that I should move on to heroin. That seems crazy, right? But with each bad decision you're judgment gets a little more skewed and obviously bad things, like heroin, sound more and more like viable options.

After taking vitals and introducing myself to my first patient, the charge nurse, Brenda, calls me up to the desk and tells me that I have a phone call. I pick up the phone and it's Mr. Braxton. He tells me to have Brenda cover my patients and to meet him in the conference room.

I hang up the phone and tell Brenda that I have to go see Mr. Braxton and that I'll be right back. She smiles and takes the chart from my hand and looks it up and down, making sure that I filled out all of the assessment information correctly. After she finishes, she looks up and nods at me to let me know that I can leave.

I walk down the long hallway with the boring pictures and find the conference room. The door is cracked and the light is on inside. I hear voices. Several voices. There is no way this is a good thing.

I walk in the conference room and Mr. Braxton is standing by the table. Four, very serious looking, older men are sitting in big leather chairs. They all get quiet when I walk in and look at me sternly. Mr. Braxton approaches me, puts his hand on my back, and guides me into one of the seats.

"Jack, these are some of our board members. They provide us with most of our funding and they like to come by occasionally to check up on things."

All of the men sit and stare at me in silence. It's very uncomfortable.

"Hello, everyone, my name is Jack Lawrence."

I stand up and reach my hand out to be properly introduced but Mr. Braxton sits me back down.

"Jack, there is something that I have not told you about us here at the Bright Futures division."

"What is that, Mr. Braxton?"

"First of all, we know about the rebels."

"Rebels? What do you mean?"

Holy shit, they know. This is bad. They're going to kill me! They're going to kill Godzilla!

"Cut the bullshit, Jack. We know. We have known about them way before you came along. In fact, Jack, we hired you because we knew that they would choose you."

"Look, guys, I didn't ask to be a part of them just like I didn't ask to be a part of you. I don't really—"

"Jack, just listen," says Mr. Braxton, as the other men readjust themselves in their seats. "We need to know everything that you know about them. What their plans are. Everything."

"That's the thing, I honestly don't know anything. They just told me that they needed some help, that's all. They didn't tell me anything specific."

"Jack, we are entering a new phase here at New Beginnings. We have developed a pill that can sterilize both men and women with very few side effects. The pill can be swallowed, or it can be crushed up and added to food or water with pretty much no taste or smell. In the new phase we will begin choosing who gets the pill and who doesn't and administering the drug without consent. There will be no more of this bribery, no more of these secret arrangements between our clients and us. We will bring people into New Beginnings and, after a thorough assessment, we will decide whether or not to sterilize. There will be no more need for any of *this* down here. The Bright Futures division will be no more. Now, what to do about all of our employees who know all of our secrets such as yourself? Well, that all depends, Jack. It depends on how willing you are to help us. You see, we believe that this group of rebels somehow knows about this new phase and that they are planning something to stop us. We can't have that happen, Jack. That would be bad for us, bad for you, and even bad for that girl that you're always smiling at, Carrie."

"So, when you start using this new pill, you're going to get rid of everyone who works down here?"

"That is correct, Mr. Lawrence. Zeus is going to be a very busy man."

The men all chuckle and look at each other.

"That is insane. You people are—"

"Watch it, Jack. Think before you speak. You're going to be just fine as long as you work with us."

"What do you want me to do?"

"We need you to find out what they are planning and who is involved so that we can stop them. It's very simple."

"Very simple, huh? Simple isn't the word that I would chose for any of this, sir."

"We are all confident that you will do the right thing, Jack. It's time you get back to your patients now. Oh, and let's keep this conversation between us, okay?"

I walk out of the conference room and get back to the floor.

I try my best to focus on my work but all I can think about are those ugly, old men and how much control they have over me.

I ask Carrie if she wants to go out after work and she tells me that she has something going on. I text Bobby and tell him that I need to go out for a drink. He tells me that he'll be at my apartment when I get home.

CHAPTER TWENTY

W e decide to go to a little bar on Davis Island where I can bring Godzilla. Bobby hands me three Adderalls when we walk into my apartment. I swallow two, snort one, and then chug a beer. I'm not concerned about my plans to get sober this weekend. Right now all I care about is drinking heavily and forgetting about everything. I don't want to think about the clinic, the rebels, or even Ben Ellsworth and his philosophy of addiction and recovery. In fact, I kind of hate Ben Ellsworth right now. Thinking about his relaxed posture and his peaceful disposition makes me angry. How dare he pretend to understand what I'm going through? How dare he try to tell me that there is a way out of all of this? That I can do something with my life. Be a better person. Fuck him and his perfect little life. That shit is not in the cards for me. It never was. My story is, and always will be, a tragedy, and the sooner I come to terms with that the better off I'll be.

I swallow three Percocets, which puts me over my daily limit, and put on Godzilla's leash. We walk outside and there is so much humidity in the air that it's difficult to light my cigarette.

We get to the bar and I tie Godzilla up to a tree outside. Immediately, three drunken college girls from a nearby table stand up and start smothering him with kisses and scratches. Bobby and I go inside to get a beer.

After we get a pitcher and take a few shots of Patron we walk outside and take two seats at one of the metal tables with the college girls. They compliment me on how adorable my dog is but I'm just not in the mood for it. One of the girls is extremely sexy and perfectly thick but I have no interest in pursuing her, even though I'm pretty sure that I could have her if I wanted her. It's unfortunate, but curvy women, at least the white ones, are taught from a very early age to hate their bodies and this usually leads to a lifetime of confidence issues. These women, who I find to be the sexiest and most beautiful, usually think so poorly of themselves that they end up with scumbags like me. Good for me, bad for them.

I look at the sexy one and think about how much fun I would have taking her home but then I think about Carrie and how I don't want to screw things up with her. She is the first person in a very long time that makes me forget about Michelle.

Bobby gets tired of looking at my sullen face and the fact that I'm not helping him hook up with women and asks me if I want to walk to his parents' house to smoke a joint. I agree and we untie Godzilla and walk to his house, which is only two blocks away.

Bobby lives with his parents in a modest, one-story house that sits below a canopy of Oak trees. His parents' cars are both parked out front, along with a boat and three Jet Skis, but he assures me that they are out for the night.

We walk into his bedroom and it's like going back in time. It reminds me of what my bedroom looked like in high school. Posters of athletes and bands completely covering the walls. Lighters, rolling papers, cigarette boxes, pipes, and scraps of paper with phone numbers written on them scattered all over the dresser. Two big speakers beside the bed that blast heavy metal music as soon as he turns on his radio. Oh, and of course there's the smell of dirty socks and incense.

We sit on his bed and he pulls a tightly rolled joint out of his nightstand and tells me that it is highly potent, medicinal-grade weed that his friend in California sent him.

He lights the joint and we each take a couple short hits and cough out the smoke. The joint is so tight that it's hard to get much smoke out of it, which he says that he did on purpose because the weed is so strong. I'm not sure if I believe him.

We take a few more hits and it now makes sense. This stuff is strong. I look around the room and I feel like I'm on a movie set. This room is just a stage prop. Everything around me, the clothes, the guitars, the posters, it all looks like it was put here by some stagehand and the lighting was fine-tuned to accent everything perfectly. Even the music playing seems like it was chosen by some director to add depth to the scene. None of it is real. It's all staged. I look at Bobby and, even though he's sitting right beside me, he looks twenty feet away. He's giggling and telling me about how red my eyes are and all of the sudden the gravity of my current situation hits me. The clinic. Oh my God, what are they doing? What am I doing? How have I gotten myself here? Dear God, I'm a drug addict. I am a drug addict. Addicted to drugs. I look down at the wounds on my arms. Holy shit, I put needles in my arms. How the fuck? This is too much.

"Bobby. Hey, I think I need to go home."

I look at Bobby and he is off in his own world. He's looking around the room with the joint smoldering in his hand. Godzilla is curled up at my feet. I hope the smoke doesn't get to him.

"I have to go to the bathroom, man," says Bobby, after he snaps out of whatever trance he was in.

"What? You're leaving?"

"Going to the bathroom, man. Calm down."

He walks out of the room and I look around. I pick up an electric guitar and lay back on the bed. I start strumming, completely unable to tell if it's in-tune or not. I turn off the radio and try to tune the strings but the notes don't make sense. The sounds don't sound right. They don't fit together like they should.

I look over at his closet, which is open and overflowing with clothes.

Something strange catches my eye.

Something sticking out of the pocket of a black jacket.

It looks like wires. Like tiny, little wires.

I stand up and walk over to the closet.

I brush the wires with my hand.

Is this real?

I tug on the wires and something black comes out of the pocket.

It's a mask. A cat mask! The wires are whiskers! Holy shit!

Bobby walks back into the room and sees me standing by his closet holding the mask.

"Jack. What the fuck?"

"Bobby. What the fuck?"

"Come here. Follow me outside."

"I'm not going with you anywhere until you—"

"Come on, Jack!"

He turns around and walks out of his room. I follow him. I leave Godzilla inside to sleep.

He walks through the back door to the backyard then to a shed by the fence.

He walks into the shed and turns on the light. He closes the door behind me after I walk through.

"Okay, Bobby. What the hell is—?"

"Shhh. Be quiet, Jack."

He turns a radio on at full volume then bends down and picks up a dirty rug from the ground. He slides the tips of his fingers between two wood planks and removes a wooden square. There is a dark hole beneath it.

"What the hell is that, Bobby?"

"Fallout shelter. Come on."

Bobby climbs down a ladder and turns on a light at the bottom. I look down the hole and see him standing there looking up at me.

"Come on, Jack. And cover up the hole behind you."

I climb down the hole and find myself in a large, illuminated cylinder underneath Bobby's backyard.

"This is an original fallout shelter, Jack. This is why my dad bought the house, I think. He restored it back to its original glory. See this crank here? This is a manual air pump. See these benches? Lift up the seats and they're stocked with enough canned goods and water to last a couple months. My dad even stocked it with old board games that they would have played back in the day."

"Bobby. This is really cool and all, but I need to know why you have that mask in your room. I'm freaking out right now."

"Calm down, man. We're safe down here. This is where Tom and I used to come to talk."

"Tom?"

"Yeah, Tom. You're neighbor who died."

"I know who Tom is. Is he part of all this?"

"He started all of this."

"What?"

"Tom was a lot smarter than he let on, man. He was brilliant, actually. He was his family's pride and joy at one point. He was going to take over some of the family businesses and handle the family fortune. He was the future of the Goodell family."

"Tom?"

"Yeah, fuckin, Uncle Tom, bro."

"This is crazy."

"He had a falling out with his father, though. His father told him all about this clinic and Tom just wasn't into it. He refused to be a part of it. He told his dad to have the whole thing shut down but of course his dad wouldn't have it. They pretty much wrote him off, bro. The whole family did. But he knew how to access the database at the clinic so he kept on top of things. He watched everything they were doing and kept track of any people who went against them and somehow got away. Then, he would find those people and recruit them."

"What about you, though?"

"Well, as you know, Tom had a bad alcohol and drug problem. He got really fucked up one night and told me everything, then, the next morning, he got all paranoid because he told me. He thought that they were going to kill me or something so we started using places like this to talk while acting like nothing had changed between us on the surface, so to speak. I wanted to be a part of it and it's not like he could say no at that point. He knew that you were going to end up working there at New Beginnings. I mean, he didn't *know*, know, but he had a pretty good feeling that that's where you would end up. He is the one who told us to recruit you if you ever started working there."

"Fuck."

"He knew about this new pill that they are developing to sterilize people."

"What was he going to do? Never mind, don't tell me, it's better if I don't know."

"He had a pretty good plan, Jack."

"No, don't."

"You and Carrie are going to get a bunch of those pills and bring them to us. After we get them, we're going to give doses to all of these old guys' kids and grandkids. We have people infiltrating all of the local private schools who are going to do it. We're not hurting anyone. Not really. We're going to do to them what they have done to the people of Tampa. We're cutting off their bloodlines."

"I have to go. You shouldn't have told me that. They know about you guys."

"What?"

"They know about you guys, they want me to help. I have to leave. We can't talk anymore. It's for your own safety."

I climb up the later and go into the house to get Godzilla, who is asleep on the floor. Bobby tries to stop me again as I leave but I don't turn around.

PART 5

CHAPTER TWENTY ONE

That was the worst weekend of my life. I ran out of pills Friday afternoon and was in a full-blown state of withdrawal by the time I got home. I told Carrie what was going on and told her that I was going to have my phone turned off all weekend. She kissed me and wished me luck.

I stopped by the grocery store and got some food and some Pepto Bismal and my hands were shaking so bad that I could barely give the cashier the money.

I got home and poured out all of the alcohol and gathered up all of the pills and drug paraphernalia I could find. I brought the drugs and syringes out to the dumpster by the parking lot and buried it all beneath five bags of steaming, rotten garbage. The smell caused me to vomit twice.

I took Godzilla out for a walk but couldn't take the sun on my skin for too long. I brought him back inside, apologized, and told him that I would take him back out when the sun went down.

Then I took a shower.

The water gave me chills no matter how hot I made it.

I dried myself off, put on some clean clothes, and got comfortable on the couch.

I put on a movie that I've seen probably a thousand times.

About thirty minutes into the movie, the spasms began.

They started mild. Little twitches in my arms and legs. I would finally find a comfortable position for my body and suddenly be jerked out of it by an arm or leg spasm. Then they get worse. My whole body started to spasm. My abdominal muscles and back muscles would contract and twist my body into strange positions. They got so bad at one point that my body was jumping completely off the couch. I could feel my muscle fibers ripping and tearing with each convulsion.

After the spasms started, sitting still was no longer an option. When I wasn't having spasms, I was rocking back and forth violently. My body needed to be in a constant state of motion. Any time I tried to stop, I would fill up with a torturous energy and it would feel like I was going to explode. I would have to scream or punch a pillow to get the energy out. I would say that from Friday afternoon to Sunday evening my body never stopped moving. Not even for a second. No sleep, no rest, just constant, desperate movement.

And the bodily fluids. Dear God. Every bodily fluid imaginable poured out of me. Vomit, piss, diarrhea, sweat, tears, drool, I couldn't keep anything in. I kept a bucket beside my bed that I would vomit and cry into for hours on end. Occasionally I would get up and sit on the toilet for a couple hours, then go back to the bucket.

I called Ben at one point and told him that I thought that I was going to die. I told him that I thought that the spasms might be seizures and asked him if he could take me to the hospital. He told me that what I was going through was perfectly normal and once again he told me to toughen the fuck up. Then, for some reason, he told me about he and his wife's plan to sell the bookstore and move to Spain. I hung up on him and got back to vomit-crying into my bucket.

The worst part was during the second day, when memories started coming back to me.

I thought about all of the women in the hospital. The ones who actually liked me. I felt so bad for them. So guilty. I thought about Michelle and all of the things that I put her through. I thought about all of the lying and stealing and the faces of the kids at the pill-mill. I thought about that video that Mr. Braxton showed me of all the deformed children. I thought about the man that Zeus shot. The man that I helped carry out to the car. The man that I watched Zeus feed to the alligators. I thought about the voice that I heard scream in the other room when Zeus shot him. Was it his daughter? Wife? I thought about the doctors and the prostitutes. I thought about Tom and the fact that he died after taking pills that I gave him. So many terrible things. Too many terrible things. I thought about killing myself a lot, but then I would look at Godzilla. The poor little guy depends on me. He doesn't know any better than to love me unconditionally.

Saturday night there was a knock at my door. I answered and it was a man wearing a black cat mask. I almost slammed the door in his face. He told me that he knew about Bobby telling me everything then he told me to look out for the new pills, which should be shipped to New Beginnings shortly. He told me to find a way to take some. I pretty much just nodded my head until he left then I went back to the couch.

I didn't even mention the smell, did I? My whole house now smells like a mixture of body odor and chlorine. The smell has permeated every surface of my apartment. I tried to clean and deodorize the place but nothing worked.

It's now Monday morning. I'm still very weak but I did get a few hours of sleep last night. I'm really having a hard time thinking about facing people without drugs in my system but I don't have a choice.

Here goes nothing.

CHAPTER TWENTY TWO

I can't think straight. People keep asking me questions and I keep zoning out as my mind searches for an acceptable response. Any time anyone makes eye contact with me I blush. I forgot how shy I am. I see Carrie walking down one of the hallways and she gives me a concerned look but keeps walking. I follow her to the supply room.

I open the door and I see her standing there holding an armful of sheets. Her face is so beautiful. I feel so unworthy. I can't believe that this woman let me have sex with her. I guess she kind of *didn't* if you think about it. I mean, was that really me? This awkward, self-conscious, blushing, sweaty person is the real me.

The person that Carrie met and slept with was nothing more than a character that I created with different combinations of substances. She's never met the real me. I'm pretty sure she won't like me.

She walks up to me and gives me a hug and kisses me on the cheek.

"You look terrible, Jack. You should be home. You look pale and swollen and sweaty."

"The way I look is nothing compared to how I feel."

"Are you in pain? Want me to get you an Advil or something?"

"No, I'm not talking about how I feel physically, though I am a little achy now that I think about it. I'm talking about the way that I feel mentally. I feel naked and small and weak. I feel like I'm living in someone else's body, someone else's mind. I don't like it. I don't like who I am, Carrie."

"You know, Jack, that's probably why you got so heavy into drugs to begin with. Instead of learning to become a stronger and more confident person, you took the easy way out and decided to let the drugs to all that for you. All the years you spent getting fucked up, you could have been actually bettering yourself. You could be that confident person by now that you've been pretending to be."

"You're right."

I have to stop talking because I can feel tears coming.

"Are you okay?"

"I'm just really emotional. I don't know why."

"Well, I'm sure you haven't felt a lot of emotions the past couple years. They're all coming up now. You never got to process any of the things that you've been through, you just stuffed them down. Those things don't disappear. Believe me, I know. Now you're going to have to come to terms with a lot of things."

"It's too much. I can't handle it. My every instinct is telling me to run away and hide somewhere."

"I'm not an expert on these things, but I'm sure what you are going through is normal. You're just going to have to see it through."

She gives me another hug and my tears fall on her shoulder. I can't hold them back anymore.

The door opens and we let go of each other immediately and act like we're gathering supplies.

Two men walk into the room. One of them is pushing a dolly with two, large cardboard boxes on it. Mr. Braxton walks in behind them and leads them to a locked closet, which he then opens. The two men put the boxes in the closet and Mr. Braxton locks the door. He gives me a smirk when he catches me watching him.

Could that be the stuff? I think it is. I look over at Carrie and I know that she is thinking the same thing. Our hands touch as we watch Mr. Braxton sign some billing slips and she grabs ahold of my finger and squeezes it. Mr. Braxton looks at us again and we both leave the supply room and get back to work.

I don't know how I made it through the day. My hands were shaking too much to open the pill packets. The damn patients had to help me get their meds in order. My face turned bright red any time anyone spoke to me all day.

I couldn't answer questions.

I smelled like chemicals and body odor.

Brenda had to repeat everything she said to me throughout the day at least twice.

But, I made it. I survived. I'll admit that there were a few times I thought about swiping a few Xanax or Valiums from the patients and just dealing with the consequences, but I didn't. And as terrible and awkward as I feel, there is a small part of myself that is standing tall right now.

I walk to my car and Zeus is parked right beside me. I walk up to my car and he stares at me through his open window. He flicks a blunt roach into the grass and asks me if I need anything.

I tell him no and he smiles at me.

He gets out of his car and I brace myself for another attack.

"I'm glad to hear that, bruh."

"Glad to hear what?"

"That you don't need nothin'. Ain't good for my business but it's good for you. You off that shit now?"

"I'm trying. I haven't had anything since Friday."

"Damn, that's a pretty good start. See, I ain't got that thing, that addictive personality thing. I can take drugs or leave 'em. Don't really make too much difference to me. Except for weed, bruh. I'd be a mess if I didn't have no weed to smoke. That other shit, nah, that ain't for me."

"I wish I could be like that."

"A waste of time to wish that you was anything you not, bruh. I could say that I wish that I was like you, but it wouldn't matter, cause I'm not. I look at you sometimes and I think about my family, bruh. I think about what it would be like to go to work every day and bring home an honest paycheck. I could pick up my daughter from school without people lookin' at me funny. I could go to dinner parties and shit with my girl without people frontin'. Hell, I could meet my girl's family, you know? Do real family shit. I ain't never gonna have none of that. My life is dark, Jack. My life is negative. It ain't no good in me, besides the love I got for my daughter and my girl. Sometimes I feel like the universe needs people like me, though. Like maybe there is a reason for me being the way that I am. If I think about it that way it's easier to deal with, ya heard? Like, maybe it ain't my fault. Maybe this is how things were meant to be. Maybe I am the way that I am to serve some greater purpose. I probably sound crazy right?"

"No, not at all. I mean, who's to say what's good and what's bad. Or who is good and who is bad. We all have our roles to play. This is your role, your character. I think that as long as you're true to yourself, you shouldn't have to feel any guilt about who you are. But what the hell do I know? My brain is fucking fried. Hopefully not permanently."

"Nah, you be alright. I seen people come off that shit before. They come around. Takes 'em a while, but they get it."

"I hope you're right."

"You know, I looked into getting some of my ink removed. The ink from my face."

"That's probably a good idea. What made you want to do that?"

"Just, the shit I was talkin' about earlier. Picturing a different life for myself. I know it ain't gonna happen but a nigga can dream right?"

"Right. A nigga can dream."

"Yo, you sound hella racist when you say that."

"You're right, sorry, I was just trying it out."

CHAPTER
TWENTY THREE

I'm outside walking Godzilla and the heat is unbearable. I hate the feeling of sweat beads rolling down my back. I hate the way my hair smells when my scalp sweats. This heat is intolerable. The only place the heat makes sense in Florida is on or near the beach. There, it doesn't seem so bad. Maybe it's the wind coming off the ocean that makes it okay. Or the mild evenings. It's so hot that I can't even enjoy my cigarette. Those are next on my list of things to quit, by the way. I don't enjoy them near as much sober.

My phone vibrates in my pocket and it's Carrie calling. She tells me that she's going to come over and spend the night tonight. She tells me that she's worried about me because I looked so bad at work today. I'm happy that she's coming but I'm also scared that she's going to be bored with the new/old me.

I take a long shower, bathe Godzilla, and tidy up the apartment. It still smells. I spray Fabreeze on all the furniture and open the windows for a few minutes to air the place out. It's better, but I can still smell it.

Oh well.

I open the door and she steps inside and gives me a hug. As she hugs me she whispers in my ear that we are not to talk about anything "work" related. I nod in agreement then I tell her not to worry about the boxes. She knows what boxes I'm talking about. I tell her that I'm going to take care of it. She answers with a kiss, and that's the end of that.

"So, how are you feeling now? Any better?"

"I kind of feel like I'm floating. My legs and arms are rubbery and weak and my head is all fuzzy. I feel like I'm just drifting along. I feel confused pretty much all the time."

"Wow, you really did make a mess of yourself with those drugs."

"I really did. I always knew that I was doing physical damage to myself but I didn't take into consideration the fact that I was altering my brain chemistry so much. I really feel like I don't know who I am right now. Like I have to get re-acquainted with myself again. It's weird."

"Well, maybe when all the dust settles you'll like who you are."

"I hope so."

"I can see the real person down there. The person that you were trying to bury. I always saw that person when I looked at you. When I met you, I saw a quiet, sensitive guy, not the obnoxious womanizer you pretended to be."

"Really? I thought I was doing a pretty good job of hiding that guy."

"You might have fooled some people, Jack, but not me. So what do you want to do tonight? Got any good movies?"

"No, but we can find one on my laptop if you don't mind watching it on the computer."

"Sounds good."

We order a pizza, eat, and then lie on the couch together with the laptop resting on my legs. She curls up against my body and puts her hand on my belly. The feeling of her hand on my skin reminds me of Dilaudid, only cleaner, and with no feelings of guilt and shame attached to it. I'm so relaxed that I don't care about the chick-flick that we're watching. My eyes roll back in my head as her fingers move over my skin. I'm in a state of pure bliss.

After the movie is over she asks me again about Ben from the bookstore.

"He was an addict. A heroin addict at one point. Anyways, he got clean by developing his own philosophy, since the twelve-step method didn't interest him. And it worked, obviously. That's what he shared with me. It made a lot of sense. I never really thought about how the twelve-step people have this monopoly over the whole addiction game. For some reason everyone one just accepts that there is that one way to do things and if it doesn't work for you then fuck you, I guess."

"That's true. That was so nice of him to help you out."

"Yeah, thank God we went to the bookstore that day, right?"

"Yeah, thank God."

"You know, he's moving."

"What? When? Where?"

"Umm, I'm not sure exactly when, but I think he's leaving soon. He's going to Spain. I guess he and his wife always wanted to live there."

"What about the bookstore?"

"Selling it, I guess."

"Wouldn't it be nice to buy it from him?"

"That would be incredible. Just kind of pick up where he left off."

"Yeah, that would be amazing. Living on top of a bookstore on the beach. Can't get much better than that."

"No you sure can't."

We stand up and she starts walking toward my room. Toward my bed. The bed that I haven't slept in since Michelle, unless you count the overdose, which I don't. She pulls down the comforter and sits down. I stand in the middle of the room staring at her. She looks so beautiful. So happy. I turn the light off and bend down to kiss her. The long kiss turns into a long night of passionate sex. She lets me cum inside of her two more times. Sober sex is so much more intense. The only problem is that it's hard to last as long without the drugs dulling my nerves. The sensations are all amplified. Everything is sensual. Her breath is sensual. Her hair. Her eyes. Things that I never thought about sexually before.

After we can't handle any more of each other, she lays her head on my chest and passes out. I can't sleep but I'm okay. It's not a bad insomnia. I'm thinking good things. Like, what if I really could buy the bookstore? What if I could marry Carrie and we could live there together? It's not possible, though, is it?

There is that one option. The option that I haven't let myself consider yet. I am a perfect candidate for sterilization. I am a drug addict. I am a criminal.

Before sunrise I decide that I'm going to go through with it. I'm going to Mr. Braxton and I'm going to ask him if I can offer him my ability to reproduce in exchange for the bookstore.

CHAPTER TWENTY FOUR

I walk into work and I have to admit that I don't feel terrible. I feel bad, don't get me wrong, like, really bad, but not terrible. Not like I want to crawl under a rock and die like yesterday. A big part of my feeling better has to do with Carrie and the fact that she still likes me. I feel a lot closer to her now. I think it's safe to say that I'm in love with her.

Would I like to have children one day? Yeah, I would, but that's a sacrifice I'm willing to make. Plus, maybe Mr. Braxton was right. Maybe people like me shouldn't reproduce. Maybe the world would be better off if people like me didn't pass on our genes. If I can get the bookstore and manage to get Carrie out of New Beginnings unharmed I think that I can make a pretty good life for us. We can always adopt if it comes to that.

Maybe I'm getting ahead of myself here.

I thought about telling Carrie my plan this morning but decided against it. I know exactly how the conversation would go. She would tell me that it was a bad idea and I would state my case and it would turn into an argument that I would end up losing. So why bother? What's the point in all the back and forth if I already know how it's going to end? It's better if I just do it and explain why later on. Hopefully she'll understand, or at least be able to come to terms with it without losing too much respect for me.

I get my morning assignment from Brenda then go pass out my morning meds. I don't even bother with assessments. These people know their bodies and what they can handle way better than I do. Brenda asks me if I'm okay when she sees me hustling from room to room and I tell her that I have to have another meeting with Mr. Braxton so I'm trying to hurry. I fill in the assessment sheets with numbers that look good and put away my charts. Brenda puts her hand on my arm as I finish up my last chart and tells me that she's proud of me. I ask her why and she just smiles and gives me a hug. Maybe she struggled with drugs herself. Maybe that's how she ended up here. Who knows? I know I'll never ask.

I walk to Mr. Braxton's office and knock on his door. He tells me to come in.

"Mr. Lawrence. How can I help you today? I hope you have some information for me."

I knew that I would have to give him something before we got into anything else. I decided to give up Tom, since he's already dead.

"As a matter of fact I do, Mr. Braxton. I found out a little bit about the history of the rebels."

"Did you now?"

"Yeah, I did. I don't know exactly what it is they're planning or anything yet, but I know how they got started."

"Let's hear it."

"It was Tom Goodell."

"Mr. Goodell's son? As in, the man who provides the largest portion of our funding?"

"That's the one."

"Interesting."

"I guess he knew about the clinic from his father but they got into some big fight about it. Tom thought that what his father was doing was unethical."

"Yes, I know all about that, Jack."

"Well, what you don't know is that when he left, he continued to have access to your computer database."

"That sly son-of-a-bitch."

"Yeah, I know. It was a shock to me, too. I always thought the guy was a burnout. Anyways, he kept on top of everything you guys were doing and started recruiting people who fell through the cracks."

"Wow. Tom Goodell. I'm impressed."

"I still don't know any of their names, but I will. I don't even know what they look like. They all wear black, cat masks when I'm around. Pretty weird shit."

"Very weird. Good work, Jack."

"There is another reason I came to see you, Mr. Braxton."

"What is it?"

"I wanted to know if I could utilize your services."

"What do you mean?"

"Before you guys make the big change and stop bribing people, I wanted to know if I could take advantage. I'm sure you know my history. I mean, I didn't end up here because I'm a model citizen. I've been a drug addict for a long time and it doesn't look like things are going to change for me any time soon."

"So, what is it you want?"

"I want to pursue my dream of owning a used bookstore. It doesn't look like I'm going to be working here much longer."

"A used, what? This all sounds familiar."

"A friend of mine owns and lives in a used bookstore on the beach and he's selling the place and moving to

Spain. I want to give you my ability to reproduce in exchange for the bookstore."

"This bookstore, it's not called Beach Reads is it?"

"Yeah, you've been there?"

"Let's just say that I know about it."

"So what do you think? Is it doable?"

"Yeah, it's doable. But if you really want this bookstore, you're going to have to be my Guiney Pig."

"Guiney Pig?"

"You're are going to be the first patient of ours to use the pill."

"The new sterilization pill?"

"Yep, I've got a few right here. We've tested them extensively, Jack, they are safe and very effective, we just haven't used one on anyone here at New Beginnings yet."

"What's going to happen to me?"

"Just some mild discomfort. Maybe some swelling and tenderness in your testicles. Nothing you can't handle I'm sure."

Mr. Braxton opens a drawer in his desk and pulls out a white pill. It's very plain looking. No numbers or letters or distinguishing marks.

"And if I take this pill, you'll guarantee me the shop?"

"I'll do you one better, Jack. You swallow that pill right now with a sip from my soda, and I'll call the shop right now and make a deal with the owner."

"Right now?"

"Right now."

I open the package and put the pill in my palm. It's dense. Mr. Braxton hands me a can of warm, orange soda.

I guess this is it. No turning back now.

I put the pill on my tongue and take a long drink from the soda can. The pill is dry and chalky and it starts to dissolve in my mouth before I get it down. It takes a few extra sips to get all of the powder out of my mouth but he was right, there really is no taste.

Now it's done. This drug is in my body, probably making its way into my bloodstream where it will then travel to my reproductive organs and render me sterile for the rest of my life. This makes me sad.

Mr. Braxton smiles as he watches me finish the soda then he looks up the number to Beach Reads on his computer and dials it on his phone.

It's obvious that Ben and Mr. Braxton know each other the moment the call is connected. Mr. Braxton asks Ben how he's doing and asks him about his move to Spain. They talk like old friends. The only explanation for this is that Ben and Mr. Braxton worked together at one point. Maybe that's how he got the bookstore in the first place. Maybe Ben really did understand what I was going through.

Mr. Braxton tells Ben that he is going to purchase the bookstore for a client and then giggles while listening to Ben's response.

"Done deal," he says after hanging up the phone.

"That's it?"

"That's it. The place is yours. You'll have to fill out a bunch of papers and all that, but Mr. Ellsworth will go over all that with you."

"Wow. Thank you, sir."

"See, I told you that we are not bad people, Jack. We are rational people. We solve problems rationally, and a lot of people confuse that with evil."

CHAPTER TWENTY FIVE

I told Carrie that I wasn't feeling well last night and that I wanted to be alone. The truth was that my balls were the size of lemons and they throbbed like you wouldn't believe. I called Mr. Braxton and he told me to take some Advil and go to bed. Asshole.

It's morning now and I feel a lot better. My balls are about back to their normal size and the throbbing has gone down considerably. I take a shower and while the water runs through my hair I have a brief and fleeting moment of clarity. It's hard to explain, but for a split second I feel like everything is going to be okay even though I know that this is highly unlikely. Even if I do end up getting killed off by the clinic or murdered by the rebels at least I can say that I beat drugs. I can say that I went toe to toe with my addiction, stood on my own two feet, and came out of it on top. Not many people can say that.

I get out of the shower and sit down at my desk with a towel around my waist. Godzilla jumps up into my lap. I scratch behind his ear and pull out the bloody canvas. I prop it up against the wall and look at it. Every splatter of blood represents one shot. The canvas is completely covered. Why did I do this? Why did I want to document what I was doing in this strange way? I thought that after I stopped using drugs I would be able to see my motives more clearly but I was wrong. There doesn't seem to be any sense to any of it.

What I need to do is figure out a plan. I need to figure out how I can get the clinic and the rebels off of my back. There has to be a way out of all of this. I just have to figure it out.

Just as I give up trying to come up with a solution there is a knock on my door. The knock is gentle, slow, and steady. The sound isn't coming from hard knuckles, it sounds like a mixture of palm and forearm, like someone is leaning against the door and pushing against it.

Who the hell could it be?

I walk up to the door and I can see Zeus's silhouette through the window. It's unmistakable. He's leaning against my door. I open it slowly and he stumbles in and falls to the ground. I step back and look at him for a second, not knowing what to expect. He pulls himself up slowly and I can see that his eyes are red and there are streams of wet tears on his cheeks. He looks at me and sees the look of confusion and sympathy on my face and he snaps. He screams and starts smashing his fists into my kitchen cabinets, reducing them to piles of wood scraps. Then, he turns around and starts punching and head-butting holes in the drywall while screaming and crying. I smell strong alcohol fumes on his breath. I grab Godzilla and back myself into the living room and stand by the other door with my hand on the doorknob. I'm ready to run if he comes after me but he doesn't. He collapses on the floor with his face in his hands. Godzilla jumps out of my arms and starts licking his face. Zeus doesn't move.

Slowly, I approach him and ask if he's all right.

No answer.

"Zeus, man. Are you alright?" I ask again.

"My baby girl, bruh," he says through the tears. "My girl and my baby girl. Both of them is dead, bruh. They dead!"

He bangs his fists into the floor and I sit down beside him. I have no words for him so I put my hand on his back. I feel the muscles contract with each sob.

"I don't know how that shit happened. We was all supposed to be going out to eat but somethin' came up and I had to stay home. They left together in my car."

He stops talking as he tries his best to compose himself. Seeing a man like Zeus this emotional is hard. It takes every bit of strength I've got not to start crying myself.

"Did something happen to the car?"

"I don't know, bruh. They crashed. They got off the road somehow and rolled. Both of 'em dead, bruh!"

He raises himself up to his knees and wraps his thick arms around me. He pulls me in tight and we both cry. And somewhere in that emotional moment, with those beefy, tattooed arms around me and the tears on my face, it comes to me. An idea.

I know how to stop the rebels and the clinic.

PART 6

CHAPTER TWENTY SIX

The first thing I have to do is get the rebels off my back. This shouldn't be too difficult. The sterilization pill that I was given looked identical to a gas-station caffeine pill, so I figure I can buy a bunch of those and pass them off as the real thing. It's not like they're going to test them out or anything. Worst-case scenario, a bunch of private school kids get amped up on caffeine and have to be sent home. Everyone lives to procreate another day.

The hard part is going to be the clinic.

And this is where Zeus comes in.

Zeus now has nothing to lose. I realized this during our long, awkward embrace on the floor of my apartment. The only thread that held him to humanity was the love that he had for his girlfriend and his daughter and now that thread has been severed. All that's left now is a mound of reptilian instincts, muscles, and prison tattoos.

So what did I do?

I gave him the purpose that he always wanted. I lied to him.

After the sobbing subsided and he loosened his grip on me I told him that I believed that what happened to his family was an attempt to eliminate him. I told him about the new plans to wipe out the Bright Futures division and everyone involved and that what happened to his car was most likely an assassination attempt gone wrong. For all I know, that could be the truth. Though, in reality, he would probably be the last to go after they used him to get rid of everyone else.

The truth is, I don't trust those old bastards. I'm certain that they have every intention of getting rid of me along with everyone else. Why wouldn't they?

I know that turning Zeus against the clinic will result in people dying but the way I see it, if those people don't die, a lot more innocent lives will be lost. People like Brenda and Carrie and all the other nurses and PCTs down there. They didn't ask to be a part of any of this. They are all people like me who just made some bad decisions. They don't deserve to die.

Do I feel bad about manipulating Zeus? Yes.

Do I think that using his tragedy to my advantage might mean that I'm a sociopath? Yes.

Do I think that Zeus will die a happy man after he kills those men? Absolutely.

After I told him about the clinic he wiped the tears from his eyes and I saw that laser focus that I saw the day I accompanied him to work.

His emotions disappeared and he immediately started asking questions.

He wanted to know when and where the board members met.

I told him that I would find out what day they were meeting and that I would let him know. Then I told him that on that day I would meet him in front of the building and give him my badge and my keys.

He stood up and walked out of my apartment without saying goodbye.

CHAPTER
TWENTY SEVEN

The store clerk at the gas station looks at me like I'm crazy when I tell him that I need a whole case of caffeine pills. He waits for a few of the customers to clear out then goes into the back to check if they have an extra case. He comes out holding a small cardboard box. He's talking on the phone to his boss trying to find out how much to charge me. He slams the box down on the counter after ending his phone call and tells me that it's going to be a hundred and fifty bucks. I brought two hundred in cash and I was worried that it wasn't going to be enough so I'm happy. I hand him the money and he gives me another odd look while ringing me up.

I bring the box out to my car and put it in the trunk.

I have to trick Carrie into thinking that I'm stealing the pills and I'm more nervous about that than anything else.

The less she knows the better.

When I get to work I see Zeus parked in the parking lot. His music isn't blasting nor is he smoking. I pull up beside him and give him a nod. He looks at me with no expression on his face. It gives me chills. I wave and he doesn't wave back. I grab a backpack from my trunk and walk into the building.

I meet Carrie at the elevator and we ride down together.

"How are you feeling today, Jack?" she asks, after giving me a secret kiss on the cheek.

"Still nowhere near a hundred percent but I'm coming around. Each day is a little better. I'm finding it easier to talk to people even though I'm pretty nervous most of the time."

"That'll get easier, I'm sure. What's with the backpack?"

I look her in the eye and don't respond. She nods her head to let me know that we're on the same page. We get off the elevator and go our separate ways.

I walk up to the nurse's station and grab my charts then I find Brenda.

"Hey, Brenda, I've got a question for you."

"What's that, hon?"

"Do those guys, the board members, do they come here often?"

"They used to not come very often, I've been seeing them around a lot lately, though. Why do you ask?"

"Just curious. Last time they were here I had to sit through a meeting with all of them. It was pretty intense."

"I'm not even going to ask what that was about. I'm just going to tell you to be very careful what you say and what you do. Those men are very powerful."

"It was nerve wracking. That's why I'm trying to find out when they're going to be here next to I can prepare myself. Last time they caught me off guard."

"I don't know if they're going to be here today but I know that tomorrow they will be here for sure. You're not going to call in sick are you?"

"No, I won't call in sick. Thank you, though. I just want to be prepared, that's all."

"Okay, then. You better get to work, hon, looks like a busy day."

I gather all my morning meds and pass them out and fill out the assessment sheets. After I'm finished with my morning routine I grab my backpack from the nurse's station and go into the supply room, making certain to pass by Carrie on my way. She looks up at me for a second then looks back down at the chart in her hand.

I go into the supply room and fill my backpack with dirty towels, wait a few minutes, and then walk out.

I pass by Carrie again and make sure to catch her eye.

I tell Brenda that I need to go outside for a cigarette. She asks if I filled out all of my sheets and I tell her that I did. She reminds me that cigarettes are going to kill me then tells me that it's okay to go. She doesn't ask about my backpack. Thank God.

I get out to the parking lot and light a cigarette. I know it's not possible but it feels like the cigarette makes me hotter. The thought of breathing in smoke from a burning plant makes me uncomfortable.

Zeus is still parked in the same spot in the parking lot.

He's staring off into space in silence.

I walk up to his car cautiously and tap on his window with my knuckle. I make sure to hold my cigarette away from his car since I know that he hates the smell.

The tinted window rolls down.

"Tomorrow," I say, as he stares straight ahead. "I'll meet you here in the parking lot tomorrow."

He just stares. He doesn't speak.

"Is that okay?"

Nothing.

"I'll be here in the morning and I'll give you my—"

"Shut the fuck up. Don't say nothin'. I'll see you tomorrow."

His window rolls up and his tires spin as he speeds out of the parking lot in a cloud of smoke.

At the end of the day Carrie tells me that she's going to stop by my apartment after she runs a few errands. I stand close to her and squeeze her ass. She slaps me on the wrist and walks away smiling.

I drive home and take Godzilla for a quick walk. Afterwards, I empty the box of caffeine pill containers on my desk and get to work opening all the packages and dumping the pills into a Zip Lock bag. It's tedious but it gives me time to think.

Okay, so, I'm going to give these pills to the rebels, hopefully tonight, get them off my back, then meet up with Zeus in the morning and give him my work badge. Then, I'm going to go to Beach Reads and sign the papers that will make me the new owner. Wait. What if they haven't paid Ben yet?

I give him a call.

"Ben, it's me, Jack."

"Jack, my man, how's it going?"

"Great. I was just calling to see if everything is squared away with the shop and everything."

"All done, buddy. How you holdin' up?"

"Good. I'm actually doing pretty good. No drugs since Friday."

"Awesome. Great to hear. You still have some tough times ahead of you but you're gonna do fine. I gotta tell you, I was pleasantly surprised when I got that phone call. I couldn't have picked a better person to hand the keys over to."

"I was surprised myself. How do you guys know each other?"

"I think you probably know the answer to that, Jack. No need to get into it. All that matters is that we're okay. We did what we had to do."

"Okay, so, I'll come by tomorrow and sign the papers. Is that okay?"

"Sure, come by whenever you want. We're packing up everything so I might need some help carrying a few things."

"Not a problem. See you tomorrow."

"See you then."

Okay, so that's resolved.

I put the Zip Lock bag of pills in my backpack and put it on my desk.

I take the empty pill packets and the cardboard box and stuff them into the dumpster just as Carrie pulls up.

CHAPTER
TWENTY EIGHT

Carrie walks into my apartment and sits on my couch. She looks concerned. I hand her my backpack and give her a reassuring nod. She looks down at the bag then back up at me.

That wasn't it, I guess.

"Everything okay? You don't have to worry about anything. We're all set."

"I'm late, Jack."

"What? Like *late*, late?"

"Yeah, *late*, late."

"I assumed you were on something since you let me—"

"I'm not on anything, Jack. I had some issues when I was a teenager and my doctor told me that I wouldn't be able to have children. Or at least he said that it was highly unlikely that I ever would. But I took a test. It was positive."

"This is crazy."

"I'm sorry. It's my fault. I feel so bad."

"Don't be sorry, Carrie. I'm not mad."

"Why? I would be if I was you."

"I'm not mad because I love you."

"You—"

"You don't have to say it back. Not right now. Just know that I do love you and I'm not mad about this. I'm actually having a hard time not smiling right now."

"You're crazy."

"No, I'm serious. Part of me is happy. Really happy. I can't think of a better person to have a child with."

"That's nice and all but I'm not sure how I feel about any of this yet. You just got clean for Christ's sake. We both work in a place that's, well, it's not where I thought I would end up. It's hard to imagine having a baby given the situation that we're both in right now. I just don't think that it makes much sense."

"What if I told you that I was about to have a career change?"

"It doesn't work that way, Jack. Not for us. The plan might work but it might not."

"What if I told you that I'm going to Beach Reads tomorrow to sign some papers that will make me the new owner?"

"How is that even—?"

"Promise me you won't be mad."

"What? I can't promise you that. What did you do?"

"I made a deal with Mr. Braxton."

"You didn't!"

"I did. I'm sorry, I knew you wouldn't agree, but I had to do it."

"Did you…?"

"Yes. I actually took one of the new pills. That's why I'm so happy about this. I thought that my chances of ever having a family of my own were gone."

"I can't believe this. This is really fucked up. So, you're going to run the bookstore and work at the clinic? That will never work."

"There are some changes coming up that are not safe to talk about right now. But trust me, everything is going to be okay."

"Are you going to live there?"

"Yeah. *We* are going to live there. If you want to."

"This is all a little fast, don't you think?"

"Definitely. But that doesn't mean that I'm not sincere when I say that I love you and that I want us to be together. And that I would love to be the father of your child."

She kisses me. I taste salty tears on her lips. She rests her head on my chest and looks at my backpack then back up at me.

"I'm taking care of that right now."

I stand up and send a text to Bobby. I tell him that I have it, and nothing else. He tells me to go to the dog beach at ten o'clock tonight.

I show up at the dog beach and the parking lot is empty. I left Carrie at my apartment with Godzilla and I'm worried about them being alone.

I look over at the picnic table and see a dark figure and a Jet Ski in the water just like last time. I throw my backpack over my shoulder and walk towards him.

He walks to the Jet Ski and I follow.

The black cat mask is as creepy as ever.

"Bobby?" I ask.

No response. If it is him, he's really in character.

Once again I find myself flying over the black water, barreling towards a drainage pipe that we seem destined to miss.

Here it comes.

The man straps on the headlight.

Almost there.

He lowers his head and I lower mine.

I close my eyes and hope for the best.

The engine echoes off the metal as we shoot through the tunnel.

When I open my eyes I'm back in the cavernous room. Two people in cat masks are standing up waiting for us and Bobby is standing behind them with his face exposed. He looks like he wants to laugh when he sees me. His face makes me smile.

"What do you have for us there, Mr. Male Nurse?" asks one of the masked men.

"I got what you asked for. I took as much as I could."

"Do you think anyone saw you take it?"

"No I don't. The only person who knows is Carrie."

"Very good. Tom was right when he suggested that we recruit you. He would be a very happy man right now."

"So what now?"

"You've done your part. We'll take care of the rest. These pills will go to our people who have infiltrated the schools. After we distribute the pills, we will have press releases ready to be sent out, which will expose the Bright Futures division and all of its contributors. We will also divulge what we have done, which we feel to be a fair punishment for their actions."

"What will you guys do after that?"

"Disappear, Jack. We will all disappear."

I look over at Bobby. I'm waiting for them to mention the fact that I told Bobby that the clinic knows about them but they don't say anything. I guess Bobby kept that to himself.

The masked men empty the pills out onto the makeshift desk and start counting them out. I ask if it's enough and they tell me that it is.

I shake hands with the masked people and give Bobby a hug then get back on the Jet Ski.

CHAPTER TWENTY NINE

As the sun comes up I tell Carrie to stay at my apartment and not to go to work. She asks me why and I kiss her and tell her to go back to sleep. She grabs my hand as I'm walking away from the bed and pulls me back towards her. I bend down and she kisses me and tells me that she thinks that she might be falling in love with me. I tell her that I'll be home early.

Before I leave the apartment I get out my laptop and go to Facebook. I click on Michelle's page and there is a whole new album of her and her fiancé. I scroll through pictures of them smiling and laughing with all of their friends and I wait for the cold rush of jealousy and regret to come over me. But nothing happens. Instead, I feel happy. I look at her face in the pictures and for the first time I'm truly happy for her. I put that woman through so much. She deserves all the happiness in the world. I think about sending her a congratulations message but decide against it. She doesn't deserve to have the past dug up, especially when she's in such a good place. She's done so well without me intervening, to interrupt that now would be selfish.

I close out the page and put my laptop away.

I pick Godzilla up and let him lick my face a few times then I kiss him back right on his nose.

I pick up my keys and cigarettes and head out.

It's an exceptionally muggy morning. Must have rained last night.

I drive to work with the radio off. I'm not sure why.

I pull into the parking lot and I don't see Zeus's car. My mind starts wandering.

Where could he be? Did he lose his nerve? Is he dead?

I look in the reserved parking spots and see a row of identical, black BMWs. I'm sure they're all here.

What am I going to do?

I look down at my badge and realize that I might actually be going to work today, which I hadn't really planned on.

What am I going to tell Brenda about Carrie not being here?

Then, I hear it. The bass. It's louder than ever.

I look in my rearview mirror and see Zeus speeding through the parking lot. Smoke is pouring out of his open windows.

He pulls up beside me. He blows out a cloud of smoke then looks at me and shows me his silver teeth. He reaches into his glove compartment and pulls out a bag of cocaine and I see him dump it out on his console.

I get out of my car and walk up to his window.

"What are you doing, Zeus?"

He turns up the music to drown out my voice. He lowers his head and snorts a towering mound of cocaine then lets out a gritty, primal scream.

He coughs out a raspy laugh and slams his fists against his steering wheel to the beat of the music.

"Here's my badge, man. The little keys here are for the elevator."

He reaches over and takes my badge then gets out of the car. He leaves it running.

"You need to get yourself far away from here, bruh. This gonna be the best day of my fuckin' life!" he screams.

I back away a little.

"Don't be scared, nigga! You ain't gotta be scared. *Them* niggas gotta be scared, bruh! Them niggas about to meet my fuckin' AK, son!"

His screaming is growing in intensity as the cocaine floods his bloodstream. He's bouncing on the balls of his feet and shadowboxing as he walks to the back of his car and opens the trunk.

In broad daylight, he pulls out two AK-47s and hands them to me.

"What do you want me to do with these?"

"Hold 'em, bruh!"

He reaches back into the trunk and pulls out two extra ammunition clips and puts them in his pockets then he pulls out a handgun and tucks it into the waistband of his pants.

He cracks his neck and bounces up and down a few more times then takes the guns out of my hands and closes the trunk.

I try to talk again but it's no use. He's in an altered state. He shoots each of his guns twice into the air and smiles at me one last time. Thick, yellow smoke is floating through the silver. Then, he takes off running toward the building.

Before he kicks open the door, he turns around and looks at me.

I see tears on his cheeks.

I can picture him stomping through the hallways firing off rounds and kicking through doors. I picture the looks on the board members' faces when they see this insane man with face tattoos barging in the conference room with assault riffles.

I look at his car, which is still running and blasting music in the parking lot.

I leave it the way it is.

I walk into my apartment and Carrie is sitting on my couch with Godzilla. She's drinking a cup of tea and reading a Kurt Vonnegut short story collection. She looks up at me and sees the anxiety on my face. She asks me what happened and I tell her that the less she knows the better. Then I tell her that we need to go to Beach Reads to sign some papers.

Ben greets us at the door, holding the black cat in his arms. I stare at him and my eyes lose focus.

Carrie is, and always was, a member of the rebels.

Carrie is the one who brought me to Beach Reads. *Insisted* we go, actually.

And Ben and Mr. Braxton definitely knew each other.

And the black cat. I noticed it the first time I came here and now he's holding it.

Could he somehow be…?

"You okay there, Jack?"

"Yeah. What? Yeah, I'm okay. Hey, we just stopped by to fill out all of the paperwork and everything. Is this a bad time?"

Ben's wife walks up behind him and wraps her arms around his waist. Her skin is olive and her hair is dark with big, bouncy curls. She's petite and curvy. Ben introduces us and she gives Carrie and I hugs and kisses on the cheeks instead of handshakes. Her name is Lola.

"I've got all the paperwork right here on the table, Jack. Once you sign, the place is yours. Of course I have a lot to teach you about running the place, but it's not too bad, you'll catch on. We'll have all of our things out by the end of the week. Now, we are going overseas so we can't take the furniture, do you want me to leave the couches and everything or should I just get rid of it?"

My mind is still wandering. Trying to put pieces together that I'm not sure even fit.

"Oh, you can just leave it. I mean, if you don't want it. What do you think, Carrie?"

"It's your place, Jack."

"It's *our* place, Carrie. It will be our place."

Ben and his wife look at me. I look at Carrie. She buries her face in my shoulder.

"Everything okay?" asks Ben.

"Yeah. We just found out that we're expecting."

"What! That's incredible, congratulations!"

Ben and Lola wrap their arms around Carrie and I and squeeze us.

In the other room we hear the television cut to a live newsfeed outside of New Beginnings.

Ben walks over to the television and turns it off.

CHAPTER THIRTY

I can't believe it's been five years. Five fucking years! My God. So much has happened I don't even know where to begin.

First of all, Milo, our son, is four years old now. He has been such a joy to have around. Teaching him things and watching him grow has been amazing. I would say that he looks like a pretty good mixture of both of us, though I like to think that he favors me more. I'm keeping my fingers crossed that he gets his mother's common sense.

And speaking of Carrie, she got a job at a special-needs school about fifteen minutes away from the shop. She really enjoys the work and the schedule will work out great once Milo starts school. Motherhood looks good on her. She's a natural. Milo comes to me when he wants to play but the minute anything goes wrong he knows who to go to. Mommy always makes everything better.

Godzilla is getting older but he has adapted well to the beach life. He spends his days greeting people at the shop and his evenings taking long walks on the beach with Milo, Carrie, and I.

As for me, I can honestly say that I've never been better. When I first got clean I had no idea what I was getting myself into. That's good, though because if I had known I probably would have been too over-whelmed to take it on in the first place. I figured I would be good to go after a couple weeks, maybe a month tops. The truth is I still feel like my brain isn't quite one hundred percent and I've got five years so-ber now. I'm a million times better than I was but I still feel like I'm recuperating.

I got into a good routine of going for long jogs on the beach every morning, or sometimes I take the paddleboard or the kayak out to the bay for a morning workout. That has probably played the biggest role in my recovery. It's nice to feel your body working like it's supposed to.

I have a few close friends that I met at the shop, fellow book enthusiasts, who take me out fishing on their boats occasionally, but mostly I just hang out with the family.

I never heard anything from New Beginnings or the rebels after that day five years ago and I don't think that I ever will. Nor do I think that I will ever fully understand exactly what it was that I was a part of. But I do believe that what happened had to happen. I have to believe that.

Ben's philosophy of addiction ended up being very helpful for me and I kind of stole from him when I developed my own philosophy of fatherhood.

I realized early on that this child is going to be much more interested in what I do than what I say. I put an image in my mind of a person that I hope that he will be one day. A person who is kind, and generous, and passionate, and creative, and healthy, and smart, and I have done my best to embody those things. I have decided to become the person that I hope that he will one day become. Hopefully it works.

So far, so good.

Printed in Great Britain
by Amazon